THE EMPIRE

Dangerous Voyage

George Mavro

The Empire Series™ Book 2

TotalRecall Publications, Inc..
1103 Middlecreek
Friendswood, Texas 77546
281-992-3131 Tex
www.totalrecallpress.com

ISBN: 978-1-59095-491-1
UPC: 6-43977-64912-6

FIRST EDITION
1   2   3   4   5   6   7   8   9   10

This is a work of fiction. The characters, names, events, views, and subject matter of this book are either the author's imagination or are used fictitiously. Any similarity or resemblance to any real people, real situations or actual events is purely coincidental and not intended to portray any person, place, or event in a false, disparaging or negative light.

I want to dedicate this book to the
men and women risking their lives
to protect this nation from
International terrorism

About the Author

George Mavro is a 24 year Air Force, Security Force veteran. He was stationed over 22 years in Europe, eight of those in Greece. He holds advanced degrees in Government and International Relations. He presently lives in Florida with his wife.

About the Book

Despite the great naval victories, the Byzantine forces have won with the help of the Americans from the future the Ottomans things still are very grim. Constantinoplis is surrounded and under siege by 70000 and huge siege canon that can knock down her walls and open a breach for the Ottomans to pour through. The young Sultan having received vital information from his American beautiful prisoner whom he has developed feelings for is poised for one last desperate gamble to capture the great city of Constantinople. It will be a do or die attempt. His failure to take the city could result in his own over throw and death.

Can General George Mavrakis with all the technology they have developed for his Byzantine allies stop the massive attack that they know is coming? If they do manage to survive what will the future be and their desire to travel to the Americas and build and empire? What does the future have in store for the soldiers lost in the sand of time?

List of Characters:

George Mavrakis: Main protagonist of novel. Commander of the American air force security and General and security advisor to the Byzantine Emperor.

Emperor Constantine XI: last Byzantine emperor and commander of Christian forces during the Ottoman siege.

Sultan Mehmet: Main antagonist. Sultan of the Ottoman Turks and commander of Moslem forces during the siege of Constantinopolis.

Zaganos Pasha: Grand Vizier advisor to the sultan.

Gustianni Longo: Mercenary commander of the 700 Genovese Italian soldiers who fought for the Byzantines.

Captain Anna Marone: USAF doctor that marries George Mavrakis.

Airman Roger Green: is part of George's security detail. He is an experienced sailor and a student of the age of sail. Helps build the Byzantine navy.

Technical Sergeant: Mat Jenkins is an air force small arms trainer and weapons smith. Will help design fire arms and cannon for the Byzantines.

Staff Sergeant Jay Burns: air force civil engineer has experience with engines designs first steam engine.

Foreword

Ottoman Camp
8 November 1452

"He was so angry at you my sultan. He even threatened to have my head shot out of a cannon."

"Now that would have been a funny sight. This is why I love you, Ismail. You are honest with me and tell me everything."

"I love you too, my brother. I would never betray you."

"I know that Ismail. Just wait and see what will eventually befall Constantine. I will soon show him who the real leader is. I will let my guns pound his walls for a few days, then when the time is right we will strike."

"You are a great leader, a conqueror!"

"Now let's have a feast and enjoy ourselves."

Gallipoli, Eastern Thrace
7 November 1452

"Admiral, there are two chests full of gold and silver coins secured in my cabin which the marines captured during the raid. There must be at least 10,000 gold and silver pieces there."

"That will be a very welcome addition to the royal treasury each common soldier will receive two gold pieces, NCOs will get five and officers 10 each as a reward for their services."

"That is good for the men's morale your majesty."

"Let's go back to headquarters and discuss our next move gentlemen."

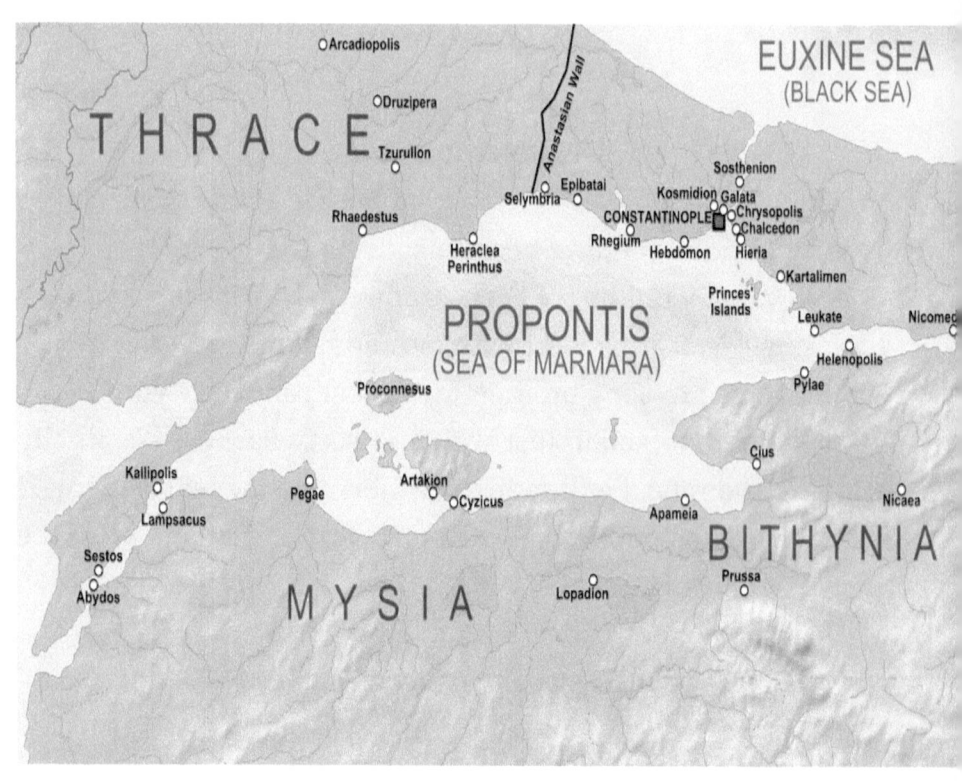

Chapter 1

Ottoman Camp
8 November 1452

The young sultan was furious and having one of his famous temper tantrums. He had learned of the destruction of the Gallipoli naval base from a dispatch rider that had been sent by the local garrison commander. He then called a council of war with all his senior commanders. The rider had arrived when the sultan had been having breakfast. One of the slave girls serving the sultan had spilt some food on him, which had been the spark to set him off. He then ordered the immediate flogging of the buxom slave girl. She had been stripped and tied between two poles. Two burly eunuchs each carrying a multi tailed whip began flogging the screaming girl on her front and back. The Sultan did not stop the flogging, until she had received almost 30 lashes by each man. When she was finally cut down she was bleeding from numerous whip cuts on her body.

"Now give this slut to my janissaries to use." She was grabbed and dragged out of the large tent by the sultan's body-guards.

"This is just the tip of what happens to those that fail me!" He yelled in the presence of his senior commanders and his grand vizier.

"I want the garrison commander in Gallipoli executed and his head on a pole for all to see what happens to incompetents!"

"Yes my padishah," the grand vizier replied.

The sultan looked to his new naval commander. "How are we doing in ferrying troops from the Anatolian coast to here?"

"It's not going very well my sultan. We don't have the ships and those we have are being attacked by enemy raiders. We are lucky to get a couple hundred men a day across."

"That barely replaces our daily loses to wounds and disease."

"We don't have any more ships, padishah. We lost two more at Gallipoli."

"I know this you fool. The audacity of them to sail into my base, kill hundreds of my men, steal two ships and over 10 thousand in gold! Unfortunately, they were able to do it very easily. The fools were all asleep. Not that it would really have mattered. That steam warship sailed right up to the beach and disgorged the troops it was carrying."

"Steam warship, my sultan?"

"Yes admiral. Why do I even need an admiral anymore? You now have the title, but no ships, except for a few rowboats and fishing boats! Seems our enemy has managed to somehow harness the principles of the scholar, Hero of Alexandria. The messenger had seen this ship leaving with his own eyes; it had paddles on each side."

"Maybe they had slaves turning a wheel with gears that turned paddles."

"So how do you explain the smoke coming out of a chimney, my brilliant admiral of the seas?"

"I can't, my sultan."

"Besides, it would take hundreds of slaves to turn wheels to power a ship its size. The ship was full of troops armed with fire arms the likes we have never seen, except what we have faced in front of the walls."

"They also have better and lighter cannon than what we have," the admiral added, the other officers shaking their heads in agreement.

"Yes, they may have better guns but we have much larger guns that can shoot a ball almost 80 times heavier then what they can and it will knock down their walls. In five days we all assault the city. We will hit them with everything we have. We will bring our guns up closer at night, then fire on the walls before day break. Once we have a breach in the outer and inner walls, we will pour the troops through there and overwhelm them with numbers. Nothing will stop us. Does everyone understand this?"

Everyone nodded their heads in agreement. "We no longer have the luxury of waiting them out. Once the Latin dogs find out we no longer have a navy, they will be here to pick up the bones, the Byzantines will throw to them. Winter is also settling in and we can't have any epidemics spreading amongst the troops. We will not give our intentions away to the Byzantines. We will continue interment cannon fire on the walls to weaken them. Now go out and make your battle plans and preparations.

Chapter 2

Aegean Sea, fifteen Miles east of the
Island of Andros
9 November 1452

The Byzantine Galleass, Aghia Maria, had left Constantinopolis a few days prior and was enroute to the Italian city state of Venice, to announce to the authorities there, the great naval victory over the Ottoman fleet. The Aghia Maria had been making good time, having favorable winds. Just east of the island of Andros the lookout had spotted many sails south west. Her commander Lieutenant Paraskevas, ordered the helmsman to change direction to intercept. If it was an enemy flotilla he would spot them with his spyglass and have enough time to get away. It could not be the Ottomans, unless they had more ships no one knew about.

Fifteen minutes later, he could make out the Venetian naval ensign on the leading ship. Within the hour they had rendezvoused with the flotilla. The Aghia Maria's captain was rowed over to the Venetian flags ship and was welcomed aboard by the admiral. "Greetings captain, I am Admiral Alvis Longo, commander of this Venetian flotilla."

"I am Lieutenant Paraskevas, captain of the Byzantine galley Aghia Maria."

"Please accompany me to my cabin for some refreshments."

The admiral accompanied by his executive office escorted

Lieutenant Paraskevas to his luxurious cabin. The Byzantine officer was amazed at the opulence, expensive silk rugs and tapestries on the floors and hanging from the bulk heads. "What brings you this way? How did you get past the Ottoman naval blockade, captain?"

"The Ottoman navy no longer exists, admiral; they are at the bottom of the sea or have been captured."

"What? How is this possible? Your navy only had a few ships. Please tell me in detail what happened."

Lieutenant Paraskevas narrated the entire siege and naval battle to the Venetian admiral, leaving out some of the details of Byzantine loses. In this world, an ally could be tomorrow's enemy. "Amazing, an entire fleet destroyed by gunfire. This is the future of naval warfare."

"Yes, sir this is the future of naval warfare and the Ottomans found out the hard way."

"Thank you for this marvelous news. We will finish the Ottomans once and for all. They are a threat to all of Christendom."

"Yes, sir,"

"Signal the fleet, we set sail for Constantinopolis. I will send a small galley to Venice with the news captain. So you no longer have a need to go to Venice, follow us back home."

"Yes, sir. I will be going back to my ship. Thanks for the assistance you are offering to Byzantium."

Constantinopolis, Royal Palace
10 November 1452

The morning staff meeting usually attended by the Byzantine supreme military commanders had started on a bad note. They had received a transmission from the underground base during the night that the base may have been compromised. Ottoman troops were now scouring the area. A squad from the mine had been sent out to hunt for wild boar but had run into an Ottoman patrol and killed five of their soldiers. Now they are searching for the culprits. So far they had missed the mine entrance. George and the staff were contemplating options.

"I thought of a plan last night while in bed."

"I would of thought of other thing, if I had a wife as pretty as yours," Colonel Longo said bringing loud laughter from everyone there.

George whipped tears of laughter from his eyes. "Even in times of crises, an Italian would think about having fun in bed."

"One must take any opportunity, because it could be his last, due to the crises. Besides, your wife is Italian."

"You made a great point there colonel and I will take it under consideration when I go to bed tonight. Humor is a great stress relief and we all needed a good laugh. In the meantime back to the war."

"Tell us of this plan, general."

"We could land a force in their rear and cut their supply lines and at the same time relieve the pressure on the underground base. The enemy would then have to dispatch a substantial force to open them back up or they would be in serious trouble very quickly, your majesty."

"That would be a very risky operation," General Mavrakis.

"It could take a lot of pressure off our walls, General Notaras."

"It could your majesty, or make the sultan very desperate and he may do something rash which either we could exploit or it could result in our demise."

"We would have to send the entire marine contingent with a couple of army companies and light artillery by sea. We can't afford to have anything happen to our base there."

"That is a good idea General Mavrakis. Admiral Laskaris can you support this amphibious operation?"

The admiral turned to his aid, an older Captain. The man nodded yes and gave the admiral a paper with the latest figures. "Yes we can. We can send five galleys, the Niki and three corvettes with two merchant ships with supplies to support you."

"We can land about a thousand men and supplies. The nine pounders can easily be disassembled and put back together. The men will be armed with flintlocks, Nagants and Ak47s.We will bring the heavy machine gun and a mortar, along with 20 shells to use in an emergency.

"And who will command these troops?" Colonel Longo asked.

"Do you want the job? You would be my first selection."

"Of course I do. Can I bring some of my people along?" They are excellent crossbow men."

"Yes I was counting on them. We have armed over 300 of them with muskets."

"Thank you. I would like to bring 25 crossbow men too. One never knows when silence and stealth is needed. They can hit a man at 50 paces."

"Your request is granted, colonel. Take what you need. You are commanding this critical mission to relieve the pressure on the underground base. Once the Turks find out about your arrival, they will concentrate on the new immediate threat."

"Thanks, general."

"Captain Jenkins and Staff Sergeant Janie Harris will also go along to handle the mortar and heavy machine guns. They will also both have radios. "Jenkins is a good man to have with you in a fight and from what I've seen from Janie she also seems very competent."

George glanced at the map. "I believe the town of Selyembria, has a small port we can use?"

"Yes, it does have a small dock. Once the marines secure the port and town, you can pull up to and unload the equipment. You will need to set up your defenses quickly. When the port is secured the local inhabitants will probably assist you in offloading the ships. We can keep you supplied by sea. It's a ten hour round trip for the Niki. The two corvettes will stay there and provide you security and gun support.

"I will manage, sir."

"We all know you will, colonel."

"The only possible threat is being eventually put into a pincer, by Ottoman forces."

"That could become a problem if the sultan dispatches forces from here, which join those besieging Heraclea. But that's what we want, to take some pressure off the city."

"We will hold them there and bleed them white, general."

"We will send the 150 musketeers we just received from Trebizond with you. They should provide you with some additional firepower."

"That will be a welcomed addition, your majesty."

"You must use your advantage wisely. They may have the numbers in soldiers; you have the fire power as the equalizer."

"When do we leave?"

"Once it gets dark, so you can hit them at daybreak."

"I know this is short notice colonel, so you must start

preparing immediately," the emperor added.

"Major Garibaldi and I will manage it your majesty."

"Fortunately, most of the required assets are here. The marines are already at the naval base and are ready at a moment's notice. You will be also given a company of my Imperial Guards."

"Thank you your majesty they are excellent troops."

"Major Tomas may make contact with you, if he believes they can risk it without being discovered by the enemy. Do you have any questions, Colonel Longo?"

"Yes, General Notaras. How long do we hold there?"

"You will hold as long as possible"

"Yes, sir. Since we will be at the backs of the Ottomans, I would like to build that bridgehead up and use it to relieve Heraclea and eventually march on the Ottomans besieging the city."

"That will definitely force the Sultan's hand, sir."

"It probably will. There are no other useable roads that he can get reinforcements and supplies for his army here. If there are no other questions, this meeting is adjourned. Colonel you have lots of work to do. Good luck and may god be with you."

"Thank you, sir."

Selybria, Eastern Thrace
11 November 1452

It was a chilly November morning in Eastern Thrace. The Byzantine flotilla had arrived during the night and had remained several miles offshore not to raise any suspicions. A mixed squad of Imperial Guards and Colonel's Longo Genovese, under the command of Captain Jenkins had landed a mile from the port, to investigate its defenses. They had found approximately 100

Ottoman irregular cavalry stationed in the small town, with very few sentries posted. Those would be dealt with right before the landings.

The blacked out Niki was drifting a mile offshore waiting for daybreak to land the marine contingent that would secure the town. Colonel Longo, Staff Sergeant Janie Harris and the Niki's captain, Commander Green, were on the bridge discussing the operation. Longo had taken a liking to the pretty young woman and had been flirting with her, throughout the voyage. Besides being very attractive, he had found that she was also a competent soldier.

"Any more reports from shore, Janie?"

"No commander, Captain Jenkins reported most of the garrison is asleep."

"Helmsman, all ahead slow, take us onto the beach. Lieutenant, signal the fleet to proceed. Sergeant, tell the captain that we are on our way. He is to take out the sentries in 20 minutes, just as we land."

Jenkins heard the order over his com., "Major Garibaldi we've been ordered to take down the sentries in 20 minutes." The major stared at Jenkins totally confused. "Don't worry sir, I have a watch. We need your crossbowmen."

Garibaldi picked two of his best cross bow men for the job. One went with Jenkins towards one of sentry's. The other man went with Garibaldi to take out the other. The first man was leaning against a wall, when the first crossbow bolt caught him in the throat. The other sentry was also quickly eliminated. The town was now wide open. Jenkins ran towards the beach just as the Niki grounded her bow on the sand. Wooden ramps were lowered and the marines began disembarking and fanning out to secure the dockside and establish a temporary defensive perimeter. Jenkins spotted Longo and went over to him.

"Colonel all the sentries are dead and my men have secured the dock. The enemy camp is 500 meters up the road. They are mostly irregular cavalry, not very well disciplined. A couple of my men are there keeping an eye on them."

"Maybe we can capture most of them and use them to unload the ships."

"It's worth a try. If we can find out where there command-ing officer is, we can possibly take him alive and offer him the opportunity to surrender."

"Let's do it, then." Longo grabbed his Genovese contingent and 50 marines and headed towards the enemy camp, with Jensen in tow. Before they could go 300 meters, they heard a shot followed by another.

"So much for surprise!"

Jensen saw the two men he had left to watch the enemy camp running towards them.

"What happened, corporal?"

"One of the officers had gotten up to relieve himself and noticed the sentry missing. He found the body and sounded the alarm."

"Guess we will soon have a battle on our hands. Marines form four lines quickly," ordered the captain commanding the company. The trained troops quickly formed four lines, rifles at the ready.

"Here they come," yelled Jensen, as the sound of a hundred horses galloping towards them reverberated throughout the small town.

The marine captain raised his sword. "At my command

prepare to fire. First line, kneeling position. Take aim." The first line kneeled and aimed their rifles at the oncoming riders.

"Fire!" Over 30 muskets spat out a .58 caliber minie ball towards the advancing cavalry men knocking over a dozen off their saddles.

"Second line, take aim, fire!" The minie balls ripped into the riders at close range several passing strait through the front targets and hitting the riders behind them.

"Third line, take aim fire!" Another dozen men were swatted off their saddles.

"Forth line, take aim fire! Begin independent fire." The marines did not have to continue shooting. The charge had been broken. Over 50 enemy Calvary riders lay dead or dying on the ground, the survivors fleeing in disorder. One of the marine officers walked over to a screaming horse that was lying on the ground, its spine shattered by a Minie ball and shot the animal.

"Well there is going to be fresh meat tonight for everybody," Longo said as he walked up to another wounded animal that was making horrible sounds. Its guts lying in the dirt having its belly ripped open by a Minie ball. Longo unholstered his pistol and put the animal out of its misery, along with its rider who had suffered a broken back.

"The survivors are going to tell their buddies besieging Heraclea that we are here, Colonel."

"You are right at that captain that's why we need to secure the town and build our fighting positions.

"We have company, sir."

Five unarmed men from the town were approaching their positions. "Greetings my friends, thank you for liberating us from the Ottomans. I am Michael Petroyiannis, mayor of this town. Who are you?"

"We are Byzantine soldiers, sent here by the emperor to liberate your town and fight our enemies."

"Byzantine soldiers, here? We haven't seen any for a very long time. You are not even Greek, you are a Latin."

"My name is Giovanni Giustiniani Longo. I fight for the emperor and Christendom, as do the men that are here with me."

"But the city is under siege and will fall soon. The Turks passed through here with tens of thousands of soldiers and giant cannons."

"Our military has so far have been defeating them. We destroyed their navy in a great sea battle, a few days ago."

"We heard the rumble of thunder coming from the sea."

"Those were the ships of the Imperial Navy and their guns destroying the Ottoman fleet."

"You have very powerful fire sticks. You have killed many of the Mohammedian dogs, who steal our food and rape our women."

"Yes we do have powerful weapons that the Turks do not have. You will see many more before this day is over."

"We would like to help you fight. I can bring 150 volunteers to join you."

"We would appreciate that very much. First we could use some help unloading the supplies and weapons off our ships."

"We will help you with that now. I will bring the men to the docks. Please take anything you need if it will help defeat the Turk. Not that we have very much left. The Turks took most of it."

"Thank you very much but we will pay for anything we take."

With the town's people's help, they finished unloading the

ships and quickly established a defensive perimeter that encompassed the entire town, which overlooked the main road to Constantinoplis. Later that afternoon, they intercepted an enemy supply convoy containing food stuff, headed for the sultan's army. The small cavalry escort had quickly been eliminated. The town people joining in the slaughter, ensuring there were no survivors. The food supplies were distributed to the townspeople who were in dire need, having had theirs looted by passing Ottoman forces.

When the sun had finally set, Captain Jenkins, Colonel Longo and Commander Green, began an inspection of their fighting positions. The Niki had pulled into the bay and dropped anchor, ready to provide gun support if needed. The three men toured the posts satisfied with what they had seen.

"We should be able to hold off a substantial enemy force, sir."

"With those nine pounders providing support and now with the additional help of the town's people, we can hold an army, captain."

"I'm sure the Ottoman commander besieging Heraclea, will send a force by tomorrow to investigate what's going on here. Even the sultan should know we are here by now."

"He probably is wondering, what to make of it. Ah, here comes Major Garibaldi."

"Good evening gentlemen. All is well at the docks. Two transports just arrived from the city with 50 cavalry, some more infantry men, food, powder stores and a few horses for pulling our guns."

"That is good news; we can use the cavalry to scout. We will be more than a thorn on the side of the Ottomans and I......"
Before Colonel Longo could finish his sentence, they heard the

sound of an engine and lights coming down the road. Several of the local militia began yelling in fear.

A half minute later, a Humvee was sighted driving down the road. "Don't worry these are friends." The militiamen calmed down and crossed themselves and said a prayer to the Virgin Mary.

Green flagged down the vehicle, the driver was Captain Rhodes in the company of four Imperial Guardsmen. "What are you doing down this way, Rhodes?"

"After you guys arrived, the Turks disappeared. We think they high tailed it back to Heraclea. The road is clear."

"That's good news."

"We heard of our naval victory. You're the new Admiral Nelson of the 15th century, Green. You love it, don't you?"

"Have to say it's pretty cool. It beats escorting convoys in Afghanistan or guarding B52s in North Dakota."

"Yeah, I guess it does."

"So what's up with you guys?

"We're close to perfecting fulminate."

"That will be a great military development for us. We'll have to remanufacture our rifles."

"I should be able to re-use the barrels."

During their conversation, both Colonel Longo and Major Garibaldi had walked up to the vehicle. "How are you Lieutenant Rhodes?"

"Just fine, colonel. We came to see you. It seems the enemy has departed our area after you all showed up this morning."

"Don't become too complacent, there are still many around and they are very powerful if they show up in force."

"Yes, sir."

"Why don't you men come down to the port and get some food. There is fresh meat, bread and wine."

"We would love some. Then we must head back to base."

Chapter 3

Ottoman Camp, Outside the City Walls
12 November 1452

The sultan had received the news of the landing late yesterday evening. Two messengers had arrived from Heraclea, with a report that the Byzantines had landed a force of a thousand men, just 30 miles to the west, severing his supply lines. He was holding court with his top commanders and advisors to discuss the overall situation. The mood in the sultan's luxurious tent was very tense. "My grand vizier, any further news on the Byzantine's landing?"

"Nothing new, my padishah, other than no supplies arrived this morning from the west."

"That was a brilliant move on their part to cut our supply lines."

He eyed his generals seeing doubt in many of their faces.

"We only have a few days supplies stocked up. As of today we are going on half rations, until we open the supply road back up. Does anyone disagree?"

"It is a wise move, my sultan, but the men will be displeased. It is winter and they need their rations to stay healthy and warm. We can't keep this up for long, we must open the road," his brother-in-law said.

"You are right my brother. We must either open the road or take this city before us and solve the entire problem."

"Before I continue, does anyone think we should quit the siege?"

"No one said a word, they were all too terrified to answer and bring down his wrath upon them."

"My Grand vizier, send word to the commander besieging Heraclea. He will to pull his forces from there and dislodge the Byzantines. He has over 2500 men with him and guns. Tell him if he fails, I will have is head."

"I will send messengers immediately, my padishah."

"Make sure you send several. We need one to get through."

"Yes my sultan, it will be done as you ask."

"My plan for this city has not changed; it has become only more important that it succeeds. Our main attack will commence in two days. The guns will be quietly brought closer to the walls during the night and we will hit them with everything we have, a couple of hours before daybreak. Once the walls have been breached, we will pour all we got through them. Mustafa Pasha, you will have the honor of leading your irregulars forward and planting the first banner on the city walls."

"That is indeed a great honor, my sultan."

"Failure is not an option. Does anyone have any questions?"

"What if the supply road is not opened my padishah?" The commander of the Janissaries asked.

"Then you will take some of your Janissaries and open it!'

"Yes, my sultan."

"Now get your men committed to this attack. This is a great Jihad against the final infidel bastion! Tell them the first man to plant a flag on the infidel's walls will receive 1000 gold pieces and great honors. Now go prepare the men; the attack will commence on the morning hours of the 13th."

Selybria, Eastern Thrace
12 November 1452

By the next day the Byzantine commanders in Selybria, had fortified their positions in lieu of the attack they knew was coming. Another shipload of troops and guns had been brought in by transports and off loaded, which helped them reinforce the landing zone even further. Except for several enemy scouts, the main enemy formation did not arrive until late that afternoon. The commander had taken the initiative to march before receiving the sultan's orders. He had in fact met the sultan's messenger enroute. He had over 2000 men with him to destroy the Byzantine bridgehead and reopen the vital supply route for the sultan's army.

When the Ottoman irregulars arrived, they were at a loss as to what the Byzantines were doing. They were expecting to be facing the enemy man to man as most battles were normally fought during that period. Captain Jenkins had instructed the men to dig fighting positions. The town had been encircled with trenches and he had the area in front of the trenches cleared to fifty meters, thus setting up a clear fire zone. In between the trenches the nine pounders were set up and loaded with canister. It would be almost impossible for an attack to breach their defensive positions. If the enemy managed to breach a position, a rapid response force of a hundreds troops would quickly counter attacker and seal the breach.

By late afternoon, the command staff was on the front line inspecting the defensive positions. Colonel Longo who was commanding the reserve force had stayed behind. It was in one of those positions, that Staff Sergeant Janie Harris found herself, when the enemy finally attacked just before sunset. Prior to the attack, the imams that had accompanied the Ottoman troops had instilled them with religious zeal for their Jihad against the infidel. Screaming Allah Akbar, (god is great) the mass of enemy troops surged forward in the diming daylight. Even though sustaining heavy losses to cannon and rifle fire they continued to advance shooting barrages of heavy arrows sprinkled with gun fire at the entrenched Byzantines who quickly began taking casualties. In the trench where Sergeant Harris was taking cover, several troops had been killed and wounded by arrows, one of the men being the lieutenant in charge. Taking command, Harris directed the defense. The next arrow barrage killed and wounded several more men. She had been firing her M4 non-stop at the advancing enemy and was almost out of ammo, but the enemy kept coming closer. "Okay men, fix bayonets; they will be in the trench soon."

The Byzantine infantry along with several of Longo's men in the trench drew their swords or fixed their bayonets to the end of their rifles and waited for the enemy to arrive. "Eagle three to command post where about to get over run." Harris said into her radio head set which she was wearing under her cap.

"Try to hold on, we're sending the reserves," Commander Green replied.

Unfortunately help would arrive too late. They had never calculated on the desperation and ruthlessness of the enemy commander, to throw the lives of his men away with wonton disregard. Having the sultan's death sentence over his head if he failed was a big incentive to succeed. The enemy commander threw his last wave at the point where Harris and her troops were defending. Despite the heavy casualties, several irregular infantry men managed to enter the trench and a vicious hand to hand fight broke out. Harris lost her cap causing her blond hair to spill out. She drew her pistol and shot one of the enemy soldiers but she did not see the one that swung the flat side of his sword hitting her on head.

It had been a close thing. Colonel Longo threw in the reserves and with the support of the guns the enemy was pushed back leaving hundreds of dead on the battlefield. The Ottoman irregulars had been badly mauled. Both Longo and Captain Jenkins rushed to the trench where Harris had been last heard from. Longo had developed feelings for the young woman after having many conversations with her the last couple of days. When they reached the trench they feared the worse. Dozens of bodies both enemy and friendly were locked in death embraces, but as hard as they looked, Sergeant Harris was not among the bodies. They were soon joined by Commander Green and Major Garibaldi.

"Oh my god they must have taken her prisoner," Longo said almost in tears.

"At least she is alive, thus there is always hope."

"One does not want to be a prisoner of the Turks, commander. She would be better off dead."

"We must try and find a way to get her back."

"The enemy had retreated and are heading east, probably heading towards their main army, Garibaldi added."

"We must let headquarters know immediately. I will go back to the ship and send a galley back to the city with a report. They should be back there in four or five hours.

"Do it commander. We must also make contact with the base and take their vehicle and try to catch up with the retreating enemy force."

"I will take a cavalry patrol and go there, colonel."

"Do so, captain."

Ottoman Camp
13 November 1452

When Sergeant Harris came too, she found herself bound hand and foot on a back of a horse heading east. She began yelling to be let down. One of the horsemen stopped and untied her and put her upright on the horse and retied her hands to the saddle. He told her if she made noise he would cut her throat. She looked around and saw that she was in the middle of a large column of enemy horsemen. The enemy commander had failed in his mission to destroy the Byzantine landing force. He thought the sultan may spare him if he brought this special prisoner to him, along with several weapons his men had captured. By daybreak they had finally reached the Ottoman lines. Janie was amazed at the size of the enemy camp. Thousands of pairs of eyes gazed at her as they traveled further inside the enemy camp. In the distance she could see the walls of Constantinopolis.

Finally after traveling over a mile through the camp, they reached a clump of large tents flying several colorful banners. This must be their headquarters she thought to herself. The pulled up to a large tent where several mean wearing turbans were standing outside. She was pulled off the horse and taken in front of a handsome elegantly dressed younger man.

"This is the prisoner?" He asked in Turkish.

"Yes, my padishah. She is also a warrior. She has killed many of my men. She was carrying this with her." He handed him the Beretta 9mm pistol belonging to Sergeant Harris.

"Take her inside, it's chilly out here."

Harris was taken inside and thrown at the young man's feet.

"She is very beautiful."

"Be careful, my padishah. She is a tiger."

Mehmet went over to where Sergeant Harris was lying with her hands hands tied. "I am Sultan Mehmet II, supreme ruler of the Ottomans. What's your name and who are you?" He asked her in fluent Greek.

She was in total shock. Never in her life did she expect to see the sultan in real life. She had heard of his temper and cruelty.

"My name is Janie Harris; I am a soldier in service of the emperor of Byzantium."

The sultan began to laugh followed by the other senior commanders present. "So the Byzantines are so desperate that they use woman against us? Your Greek is much accented. Where do you come from?"

"I come from a land very far away."

"Where is this faraway land?"

She did not answer him. "What is this strange weapon?" He pointed it at her and others.

"Be careful it is a gun. It can kill very easily."

"How does this gun work? Where are the lead balls?"

"They are loaded in the weapon. Press that button."

The sultan pressed the magazine release and the magazine dropped out. Mehmet picked it up and looked at it. "So these are the super weapons that have been killing my soldiers." The sultan put the magazine back in the gun.

"So how does it shoot?"

"You point it and pull the trigger."

"Hmmm. Commander, it was very wise of you to bring this valuable prisoner to me along with this weapon."

"Thank you, my padishah."

"But you still failed me. You failed to reopen the supply road and destroy the Byzantine landing."

"But I tried, my padishah. They were very well armed, much better than us. They all had fire arms and many cannon."

"You still failed me and I did say I would have your head. Well so be it." The sultan pointed the pistol at the commander's head and pulled the trigger. The pistol fired a bullet into the man's head killing him instantly.

"Be careful the gun is cocked and will fire again if you squeeze the trigger. See the hammer in the back of the pistol. It is cocked back and will fire with a very slight pull."

The sultan looked at the gun. "This an amazing weapon. So tell me what I do next?"

She gave him instructions on de cocking the pistol. "So how many shots can this gun fire when full?"

"Fifteen shots."

"How far can it shoot?"

"About 30 paces accurately."

"Do you have any more ammunition for this weapon?"

"No I don't."

"Search her."

Two of the sultan's guard searched her and found two more magazines. "Here are two more my sultan."

"So you lie to me. How many of these weapons and the larger ones do you have for your military?"

"I don't know?"

"She needs to have her tongue loosened. Strip her."

The guards quickly removed her cloths. "We found this on her, my sultan."

They gave her communications device and radio to the sultan.

"Another toy from such a pretty creature. Tell us what this is," he said as he admired her beauty.

"Tie her to the bench and give her fifty strokes of the cane on her soles. I do not want her beauty marred."

The guards tied her to the bench with her feet exposed at the end. One of them picked up a long thin cane. "Begin."

She heard the swish of the cane and felt a searing sensation at the bottom of her feet. She tried not to scream, by 20 strokes she was screaming at the top of her lungs, by fifty she was being driven insane by the pain. "Give her ten more."

After they had completed the last ten she was crying in pain.

"Now if you want the pain to stop, will you tell us?"

"I don't know anything."

"Use the whip, but do not break the skin. Fifty strokes front and back."

The guard untied her and roughly tied her on her tiptoes. Both guards picked up a leather multi tailed whip which was designed to punish errant haram girls and not cause damage to their bodies.

"Begin."

She heard the swish of the whips and felt the searing pain as they connected with her skin. Her back and front was on fire. She passed out at 40 strokes. "Wake her."

One of the guards threw some water on her face, waking her to only continue her torment. By fifty lashes she was striped almost everywhere with welts and bruises, but she was basically not damaged. "Will you tell us my dear before we really have to hurt you?"

"I don't know anything, please stop."

Mehmet nodded and one of the guards picked up a small

metal rod that had been heating in the fire that was keeping the tent warm. He approached the hanging girl and barley touched it to her buttock. She screamed and passed out. The guard threw some water in her face, "Now I want these unpleasantries to stop, will you tell us or he will touch your breasts with it." He was bluffing, he would not mar her beauty but she did not know that.

"Yes, I will tell you. I don't know very much though."

"Good that is a start. "How many of these weapons do you have?"

"Maybe, a bit over a hundred."

"Where did they come from?"

"They came with us?"

"Where are you from?

"From far away?"

"Still playing games?" The sultan nodded his head and two of the guards carrying single tailed whips proceeded to give her ten more strokes.

"Please stop. We come from across the Atlantic Ocean, from a land called America."

Mehmet thought back and remembered some maps he had once seen drawn by the ancient Greeks that showed a landmass to the west. "How many of you are there from this America."

"There are sixteen of us."

He went and picked up her communication device. "What is this thing I am holding?"

"It is a device that enables us to talk to one another over short distances."

"How is this possible? You are lying. Give her ten more."

"The guards began to lash her again. "Please believe me. We are from the future."

"Stop! Now all of you get out now. Out!"

The tent quickly emptied. Mehmet cut the girl down picked her up and carried her gently to his bedroom area. He put a goblet of wine to her lips which she drank greedily.

"Thank you."

"I did not want to do this. You forced my hand. I am desperate and fighting for my survival here; my own people will try to have me killed if I fail to win this battle. If I die so will you in their hands."

She looked in his eyes and could tell that he was telling her the truth. He poured some water in a bowl soaked a cloth and wiped her face.

"So you are from the future. That explains a lot of what's been happening, like the steam propelled ship and the advanced weapons you have. What year did you come from?"

The girl began to shiver. He put her under the fur blankets to keep her warm. "We came from the year 2015. We were soldiers fighting Islamic jihadists in Afghanistan. We were attacked and fled to an underground mine. A suicide jihadist blew himself up in the entrance and trapped us there. We went deeper into the mine and found an underground military base that had been left their by the Russians. They were doing time travel experiments. We activated something and here we are."

"The Russ?"

"They are called Russians in my time. They were a great military power and empire after the 2nd great world war.

"Second great world war?"

"Yes there were two great world wars that engulfed the entire planet and killed tens of millions. During the second war fought from 1939 to 1945, men fought in the sky in great metal flying machines. They flew hundreds of miles to drop bombs from above and destroyed enemy cities. Finally the ultimate weapon, a super bomb an atomic bomb was invented that could wipeout a city with its use. Those weapons could also destroy all of mankind if used in mass. Fifty million died in that horrible war."

"Unbelievable! One bomb that can destroy a city and kill tens of thousands. Bombs that cand destroy all of mankind. In the name of Allah, that is sheer madness."

"We almost destroyed ourselves a couple of times."

"During the first world war which was fought from 1914 to 1918, the Ottoman Empire was defeated and it collapsed."

"An Ottoman Empire?"

"Yes, you were supposed to conquer Constantinopolis next year in May and create a great empire that would last for 500 years. You would have gone down in history as Mehmet the conqueror."

"A great empire and I would be known as a conqueror. So history has been changed with your arrival and intervention. In the name of Allah, what will happen now? Please call me Mehmet," he said as caressed the girls head.

"I do not know, Mehmet, everything has changed," she said

Mehmet gave her some more wine and pieces of fruit. He had never seen such a beautiful creature with golden hair.

"You said that you were fighting in Afghanistan against jihadists? Were these new crusades against Islam?"

She told him about 9/11, the rise of radical Islam, Osama bin Laden and the Taliban

"Allah, please forgive us for our sins! Moslems will be flying great flying machines into buildings almost 500 paces tall and killing thousands of innocents. What madness! So Islam will be perverted by evil men and Christian and Moslem will once again be pitted against each other, 500 years from now."

"Yes Mehmet that is what happened. We were fighting for ten years in Afghanistan against the Taliban. Right before we got here, a radical new movement, composed of thousands of radical jihadists, captured a large swath of territory from Syria and Iraq, what you now call Mesopotamia. They founded a new caliphate in this area calling themselves the Islamic State of Iraq and the Levant. They did this through sheer terror, murdering and torturing thousands of Shia, Christians and even Sunnis who did not agree with their radical views. They burned people alive in cages all in the name of Islam." She could see that Mehmet was deep in thought. A coalition of Christian and Moslem states was being forged to fight them."

"If I capture Constantinopolis, I will not force the inhabitants to convert. Islam is not to be forced on anyone. Only those that truly want to embrace it in their hearts can do so. One must desire to accept the word of the prophet."

She looked at him questioningly. "What will you do with me? Kill me."

"I will do no such thing to such a beautiful creature," he said as he stroked her brow. She smiled at his kind words.

"Here have some more to drink and eat." After her third cup of wine she was very lightheaded.

"What will you do now that you have this knowledge? It will be very difficult if not impossible for you to take the city. They are extremely well armed."

He took her hand and kissed it. "I know you told me much more then you needed. I thank you for it. As I told you before I don't have a choice. I must take this to a final conclusion or those wanting my throne will try to kill me. I will call one of my slave girls to put some salves on your welts. There are not many, I didn't want to damage your beauty. "

"No, I do not want anyone else to touch me except you." Mehmet took the salve and began applying it to her welts. His touch was so exciting. After a while she grabbed his arm and pulled him to her. Even though she was sore from the beatings, she was so aroused and enamored by this man withsuch great power. After they had finished, he lay next to her. She had fallen asleep on his shoulder. He had many women in his days but not like this one. She had drained him.

Finally he got up. "I must supervise the final assault on the city. It begins tomorrow morning."

"Please Mehmet don't do it. You may lose your life. They have more modern weapons in the city that they have not even used. They have a powerful armored chariot with a cannon and machine guns mounted on it. It is called a BMP and was found in the Russian base. It will slaughter your men if they go near it. Nothing in this time can destroy it."

"I will lose my life anyway, if I don't do anything. My own men will depose me. I don't have a choice."

"Then have a retreat planned into Anatolia. We have a saying where I came from. He who runs away, lives to fight another day."

Mehmet thought about what she just said. "That is a very wise saying and I will take it under consideration and plan accordingly. Now stay here, I will be back."

"Wait." She went over picked up her pistol put it in the holster and then put the gun belt around his waist. "Wear this. It still has 13 shots. It is also a symbol of power." She then kissed him on the lips. "Now do what you need to do and come back to me."

Beside this woman being very beautiful, she was also very

wise he thought to himself as he headed towards the grand vizier's tent. When the sultan walked in the man was having a cup of flavored tea. "My padishah, this is an honor."

"Listen closely to what I have to say, Zaganos Pasha. Your life is also at stake here if we fail tomorrow. I want you to plan for our retreat, if the attack fails and it may. I want you to send, a very trusted man up the straights and find as many boats as he can. One way or the other we will both survive to live and fight another day. We will use them to cross into Anatolia. I will take as many Janissaries with me as we can evacuate across the straights."

"Yes, my padishah!"

"Do not tell anyone else."

"What did the woman tell you?"

"Many things about the future, my friend."

"I will get started at once, my padishah."

"One other thing. You will send a messenger to make contact with General Mavrakis and tell him that I have Janie. You will demand that he gives me extra ammunition for the Beretta pistol and another rifle weapon with ammunition or I will torture her to death and send him the body."

His grand vizier looked at him with dread. "I am only bluffing. I really like this woman. No harm is to come to her whatever happens."

"Yes, my Sultan."

Constantinopolis
13 November 1453

It was late afternoon when George had received word of what had befallen to Sergeant Janie Harris and he was now, beside himself. He was pissed at Longo and the rest of the commanders over there, for letting it happen. He thought for a moment. He could not solely lay the blame on Longo, the man was suffering enough. It was obvious that he had feelings for the girl. This was war any anything could happen to anyone. It was his fault too. Janie should not have been there, but she had insisted that she wanted to see some action and gain some experience. Anna had not been told yet. She would not take this very well. There was a knock at his office door.

"Come in."

"Sir there is an Ottoman messenger at the gates, flying a flag of truce. He said he had a personal message from the sultan for you. We brought him here."

"Show him in."

The Turk was not a soldier nor was he armed. He looked like he served as a bureaucrat. The man bowed when he saw George. "Greetings esteemed general. My name is Ahmet Ali. I work for the grand vizier. The great Sultan Mehmet II has a message for your ears only.

"What is it?"

"He said that he is holding the blond woman Janie as his prisoner. He requests that you send him bullets for the small gun she was carrying and also one of your long guns that can shoot many times with bullets. If you do not meet his request he will have the woman tortured to death and send you the body."

"What? You animals!" he pulled his pistol and put it at the messenger's head. The man began to tremble from fear. "I should kill you and send your body back, but you are only the messenger. How do I know she will be safe?"

"The sultan gives you his word."

"I will give you what he wants. If he harms the girl I will personally hunt him down and kill him with my own hands. Tell him that."

"Yes general, I will.

George called in one of his bodyguards and gave him instructions to go the armory and prepare for him to pick up six boxes of 9mm rounds and an AK47 with a case of a thousand rounds. After the guard left George turned to the man. "I have a better idea. I will take you back personally to the sultan under a flag of truce. I want to see her."

"I can't guarantee your safety."

"We will ride in my steel chariot. It can spit out hundreds of bullets a minute and kill all those that attack it. Now let's go."

They walked to the armory where the Humvee was waiting, with Sergeant Davis in full US air force combat gear manning the M240B machine and Master Sergeant Thompson in the passenger seat carrying an M4 with a grenade launcher. There was a large white flag flying from the roof. The Turk was terrified when he was told to get in.

"This thing is from Satan, I will not get in it."

"George pulled his pistol and put it on the Turks turbaned head. "If you don't get in, I will blow your brains out."

The Turk got in and they drove to the City gate where an escort composed of ten Sipahi cavalry men, were waiting for their charge. George stopped the vehicle and he could see sheer look of terror on the soldiers faces. "Tell them Ali, that we will accompany you with the sultan's gifts. I will personally deliver them. If they make the slightest threatening move, they will all be killed. Tell them this is a machine of death."

"How do I know you will not harm the sultan?"

"I give you my word of honor, just as I believe the sultan's word that he will not harm his captive."

"I accept that."

"Tell the officer of the detail to lead the way we will follow him."

The man was let out of the vehicle and walked up to the officer in charge of the escort and told him what the new plan was. The officer looked worried, but Ali raised his voice and the officer agreed. The Turkish official got back into the Humvee and the Sipahi escort in a slow gallop, led the way towards the Ottoman lines. When they reached the Ottoman encampment the three Americans were shocked at the thousands of tents, soldiers, wagons and humanity it encompassed. They saw thousands of camp followers, composed of women and merchants with their wares. Many of the soldiers either stood in awe looking at the Humvee as it passed by or ran away in terror, screaming for Allah to save them from the Djinn. George also noticed that many of the troops were gathered in larger formations training.

Finally they reached the sultan's encampment that consisted of several large tents, with at least a company of elite Janissary infantry armed with fire arms, swords and crossbows, providing security. When the Janissaries caught site of the Humvee approaching, they rushed towards the sultan's tent ready to lay down their lives to protect him. The Sipahi commander stopped his troops about 100 meters away and galloped up to the Janissary commander to brief him. George looking through his field glasses noticed that the Janissary commander began berating the cavalry officer. The argument quickly ended when a younger man dressed in splendid armor, stepped out of the tent, carrying what looked like a jewel encrusted sword. Both men stopped arguing and came to what looked like attention. The young man glanced at the Humvee and walked towards it.

Instead of fear, George saw surprise and curiosity on his face.

George drove forward very slowly for another 50 meters, stopped the vehicle and got out as the younger man who had to be in his early twenties approached. "Well, well what a surprise General Mavrakis, so this is a Humvee and that is a machine gun on the top of it." George was suddenly dumbstruck, especially when he noticed the Beretta strapped to the young man's side.

"Oh how rude of me. I am sultan Mehmet II. Welcome to my encampment. Don't worry about your safety; you are here under a flag of truce. Under Islamic law you are my honored guest and afforded protection. Besides, I do not want to find out what damage that machine gun can do."

"Enough of the small talk Mehmet. I brought you what you asked for, now want to see Janie." George motioned to Thomson who unloaded the ammo and the AK47 rifle. The sultan had one of his men take the weapon and ammo away.

"General, please all in time. Let's go into my tent for some food. I would love to talk to you."

"I don't have too much to say to you other than if you harm the girl I will personally kill you."

"General, you should be more polite towards your hosts. You Americans are so crude. You will need to learn the eastern ways to survive here. Besides I am rather fond of the girl, I would never harm her."

George was even more surprised. History did say that Mehmet was very educated and intelligent. What he just heard proved that beyond a doubt which made the man even more dangerous. "You threatened to torture her to death."

"I had to make a credible threat to get the ammunition and the rifle. Now please join me inside. Janie is there. You can bring your men; no one will touch a hair on your head that is my word. It is also Islamic law. We are not the Taliban or ISIS!"

That really shocked George. This man knew everything about them. "I trust your word, Mehmet, but one man will stay with the Humvee, they can take turns guarding it. This is how we do it in my military."

"As you wish general, but there is no US air force, at least not for another 500 years," said the sultan as he began to laugh.

"Well maybe you now have a Byzantine air force of hot air balloons," he said laughing even harder.

"It may be a lot sooner than you think, Mehmet." George said as he thought about the engine blocks, back at the underground base. He wondered if the sultan knew about that.

"Leroy, you are the lower ranker so you take first shift. It they try anything funny open on them then get out of here."

"Yes, sir."

The sultan turned to his officers and told them to stay outside. "Please accompany me inside and don't worry you are safe."

For some reason George believed him. Islamic law and customs were very strict when it came to the treatment of guest, even in time of war. George and Master Sergeant Thompson followed the sultan and his entourage inside the huge tent. They were amazed at the opulence, priceless Persian rugs covered the floor, silk and gold lamps and decorations filled the inside. In a corner of the tent he saw Janie Harris sitting on large fluffy pillows. She was dressed in middle astern garb and was wearing a fur jacket. When she saw George she got up and hugged him. "Janie, are you okay?" George asked her in English.

"Yes, I am fine," she answered in Greek.

"See, I told you general that she is okay. Now please sit and enjoy some food and refreshments." The sultan clapped his hands and servants came over with golden bowels filled with nuts, raisins, dried figs and dried and salted meats. Others came with golden goblets that were filled with wine.

"Please have some appetizers before the main course. "

"Thank you, we will."

"So you see, Janie is safe and actually I think she enjoys it here with me. She is welcome to stay."

"Well Sergeant, what do you have to say?"

She looked at Mehmet and George could see that she had admiration in her eyes and so did the young sultan. He did not know what had happened between the two but they were both about the same age. Love strikes in mysterious ways. But why did it have to happen now and like this.

"I choose to stay with Mehmet, if he will have me."

The young man's eyes lit up with happiness or lust. Maybe both, George thought. "Of course I will have you."

"Okay, at least I know you are safe for now and happy."

"Thank you, sir." She came over and gave him a hug and a peck on his cheek.

"Don't call me sir, anymore." My name is George. You are officially discharged.

"Well that settles it general. I don't suppose I can convince you on peacefully surrendering the city?"

"I was going to ask you almost the same thing, Mehmet."

"So war it must be then. But let's talk about other things. You have altered history and denying me my place in it! I would be known as Mehmet the conqueror, had you not shown up."

"We did not choose to come here."

"That is true. It was the will of Allah. What he commands is to be. What the future has in store for all of us, only he knows."

"We will see what happens, Mehmet. The world has been altered forever with our coming. There are new weapons of war and steam power. We will use steam for the betterment of all mankind. It will take us to America."

"That is if you defeat me."

"Those are my intentions."

The servants walked in with plates of roast lamb, rice and vegetables and laid them in front of everyone so they could help themselves.

"We will take your Russian base once the city falls and use the knowledge we gain from it to build a great Islamic Empire. I will not allow Sufism and other sects of Islam to exist. Thus there will be no Taliban and corruption of Islam.

"Good luck on that. My world is a mess because of Islamic extremism. The Ottoman Empire was partially responsible, along with the western colonial powers. The Ottomans contributed nothing in the ways of economic growth or education. No great universities or centers of learning were built and very little infrastructure was constructed in the lands they occupied. You lagged far behind Europe. You collapsed from wars with the European powers, internal decay and corruption."

"Now that I know all these things and have a great advisor, things may turn out differently. My future decedents will not send our armies to Vienna, to be defeated," he said clasping Janie's hand.

"As for the Russian base, Mehmet, you will not be able to do much with it. The technology is just too advanced for you."

"We will find Byzantine craftsmen that will be greatly rewarded if they work with us."

"The problem is that there is no technological base to use what is there. It will take many years, even centuries to develop some of the things needed, such as metal working, chemistry and engineering."

"I will open universities and invite the brightest minds in the world to study and teach there."

"I suppose there will be some progress made in science and engineering and in the weapons of war, which is normal for humanity. In my time, we reached the capability to destroy all life on this planet."

"It is a miracle that you have so far not destroyed the world with your atomic bombs in your time line. We have seen how your advanced weaponry is very efficient killing machines. They have so far really made a big difference, but you have finite resources and I have numbers."

"We will see. I still have some surprises, Mehmet."

"What your mortars? It is a very interesting weapon and I love calculating ballistics. We will construct some too, in the future. You almost killed me once with them. Unfortunately, you don't have enough bombs for them. But you do have your secret weapon, the Russian BMP."

George was furious that Janie had told Mehmet all these things. But since she committed to him she would have to ensure he stayed alive.

"That too, Mehmet."

"My men will throw themselves by the thousands in front of it in the name of Jihad. It will be trapped and unable to move then we will burn it."

"Many hundreds of your men will be killed, if they attempt to do that."

"I have tens of thousands to spare."

"I have a proposal. Take your army and leave. Cross the straits and take Asia and the middle east. We can than live in peace. I am sure the emperor would agree with me."

"I can't do that. My capital is in Edirne. I will be deposed or killed by my own men. We've sacrificed too much. The war goes on to a conclusion one way or the other. Plus, I want your ship yards. We need to build large ocean-going ships, to go to America."

George understood what he meant. He knew Ottoman history. Mehmet was too new on the throne; He could not survive, if he gave up the siege. "I suppose if I were in your place I would do the same thing at this point. If you do manage to take the city, don't sack it."

"I will see. I must reward my troops somehow. I will ensure there is religious freedom in my empire, so Moslem and Christian can live and work side by side in harmony."

George glanced at his watch. "We must go back to the city. Thank you for letting me see Janie. Take care of her and listen to her whatever happens."

"I will listen to her advice and yes, I may lose, but I may also win."

"We will fight you to the last man if we have to."

"Whatever is the will of Allah, will happen."

"That is true; it is up to god to decide the victor."

"Now may I ask a favor?"

"Sure."

"Can I look in your Humvee?"

Chapter 4

Constantinopolis
12 November 1452

True to the sultan's word, after giving him a ride in the Humvee they were escorted through the Ottoman lines and back to the city. George immediately went to military headquarters called a meeting and related what had occurred. Present were the chief of Staff General Notaras, General Perdakis the army commander, Admiral Laskaris and the emperor. George was getting admonished by both the emperor and General Notaras.

"You all could have been killed. It was very foolish what you did."

"It was your majesty, but I had to know if she was okay. Anna would never have forgiven me otherwise."

"Neither would Mary forgive me, if we did not find out about her fate."

"She's joined him and he knows everything about us. I must admit, he is a very intelligent young man for this period."

"She is young and infatuated with him and so is he. He is well educated in the Greek classics, science and math."

"I wish we were not at war with him. With Janie at his side he could be a valuable partner."

"Would never happen, he is Moslem and we are Christians and he is seeking to build an empire," Notaras said.

"And that is why I believe gentlemen that an attack is imminent. I saw what looked like preparations in the various camps and now that we have cut his supply lines they must attack. Their only options are to go for broke here or attack our bridgehead that is cutting off his supply lines, or starve. I suspect he will attack very soon."

"That is very possible and we must be prepared," General Perdakis said

"We will double the troops on the walls facing them and have our response forces stationed between the walls and ready to move at a moment's notice."

"Good point, General Notaras. In my timeline they knocked down the walls and found an open gate that helped them enter the city. When your troops saw the Ottoman banners on the walls, they panicked and left their posts, giving time for the enemy to reinforce their positions and bring in more troops."

"This time we have troops with rifles and artillery in between the walls in case they do break through."

"I'm sure he knows by now what happened in your time line. We are in a much stronger position though anything is possible."

"That is true your majesty. I suggest we keep the BMP ready and the woman close by, if we have to evacuate."

"Good suggestion, I hope they listen. Both of them are working at the hospital."

"I will order them to leave and forcefully remove them if we have to. I want all your people and important equipment in that vehicle. If this city falls you will break out and head to our bridge head. Admiral Laskaris will evacuate as many troops as possible and head for there. We will destroy the Russian base and head for the Peloponnese and establish ourselves in Greece. Maybe we even head for America."

"Yes your majesty, hopefully we will never come to those choices."

"If I fall, General Notaras and General Mavrakis will rule as regents until my child is born. Yes, they empress is with child."

"Congratulations, your majesty," George said.

"Save it for later. Now go prepare."

"I'm going to the hospital."

"Maybe you can talk some sense into them."

"I will give it my best shot."

Fifteen minutes later George reached the hospital with his entourage of body guards, it was late in the evening and most of the patients were asleep. George went to Anna's office where he found both women. Anna went up to him and punched him. "You could have all been killed you idiot."

"We would have taken many of them with us. Besides they do have an Islamic code of honor towards guest."

"How is Janie?"

"She is doing great my empress."

"Cut the empress crap George and tell us about Janie."

"She wants to stay with him. She is infatuated with him and for now, so is he. She also told him everything about us."

"She is in love and trying to protect him."

"Well she kind of screwed us in the process. He knows about the Russian base, he knows about our weapons and he is now very desperate."

"Desperate men do desperate things."

"You are correct, Mary. I do believe that he is getting ready to throw all he's got against us in one desperate gamble."

"You couldn't get him to call off the attack and live in peace?"

"No Anna, his own men will overthrow and kill him. There is also only room for one empire here at the moment."

"So it will be war?"

"Yes it will be war. That is why I want both of you to be at the palace close to the BMP 1. We will use it to evacuate to the west if the walls are breached. It's being fueled and loaded with all our equipment. The Humvee will follow. We will meet up with the bridge head we've established and go from there."

"No, we will stay here and treat the patients."

"No you won't Mary. If something happens to your husband you are carrying the future emperor or empress and you Anna, are carrying our child."

"I didn't know you're pregnant?"

"I've only know for the last couple of days."

"You can't stay here. For once George is right, if anything happens to Constantine and you, the dynasty is lost. We both will go."

"Good. I have a carriage outside waiting."

Ottoman Camp
13 November 1452

The sultan had summoned his key officers for a last minute conference before the attack was to commence. This would be it, the city must fall today. He would throw all his forces in one mighty attack. The big guns had been brought closer to the walls aided by the fog. He had told his commanders about his meeting with the Byzantine-American general and who he really was and where he came from. This way his men would know the weapons were all created by men and not demons like many of them thought.

Mehmet glanced at the watch that Janie had given him. "We

will attack in two hours; the guns will hit the St. Romanos gate. It has been weekend by continuous gun fire and that is where in another time we succeeded in entering the city. There is no reason we can't repeat our success."

Janie had her IPAD mini with her in her kit bag, which had also been captured. She had installed several historical programs prior to deploying to Afghanistan. One of them had a chapter on the fall of Constantinopolis which she had shown to Mehmet, after General Mavrakis had left.

"When the wall is breached Mustafa Pasha will lead the first wave. Your men will have to deal with the troops that are deployed between the inner and outer walls."

"I am very honored, my padishah."

"The guns will be moved closer and bombard the inner wall to bring it down."

"After that the provincial troops will fallow. They will carry barrels of powder that will be planted at the most damaged points of the wall, to blow larger holes. My Janissaries will then attack. I will be at the front."

"My men are ready to die for you, my sultan."

"I do not want them giving their lives foolishly, they will not charge straight into cannon fire. They must take the walls and get into the city and open the gates. The must fight intelligently and outwit the enemy."

"Yes, my padishah. I will relay your orders.

Mehmet was keeping half his Janissary force in reserve, along with a unit of Sipahi to make good his escape if his plan failed. He had also spoken to his brother-in-law and wanted him near-by. He would need him and his troops if they had to cross over into Anatolia.

"Let our soldiers know that the first man that plants our flag on the walls, will receive great riches and titles. Now go prepare your men. The attack begins in less than two hours."

Mehmet waited till all the commanders had left. "So have you made the arrangements my grand vizier?"

"As best as I could at such a short notice. There will be 20 to 30 boats in various areas down the coast by Tharapia, a fishing village about 8 miles from here, to take us all across to the Anatolian side."

"Let's hope we don't have to use them, but we must be prepared. Now go and continue with your preparations in case we must flee. Not a word to anyone."

After the grand vizier had left, Mehmet walked back to his bedroom area where Janie had been waiting. "Everything has been set in motion. What Allah has predetermined will happen. Our fate now is in his hands."

"Be careful, Mehmet."

"You will, stay with my grand vizier, he will protect you."

"I will be with my troops, the attack starts in an hour. I have a surprise for them, a page from the future."

"Take the rifle, Mehmet."

"No you keep it for protection. I will have the pistol. He kissed her and walked out of the tent where his body guards were waiting.

Constantinopolis
13 November 1452

It had been a long night for everyone on the walls. George and General Notaras were making their rounds on the inner walls trying to keep the troops morale up. They had been hearing sounds all night but due to the heavy fog they could not see anything. Occasionally they fired a few salvos of shells at the noises. Something was up, but no one knew what. The sun would be rising in less than two hours.

"The men are on edge, George."

"They hear all those noises. The Turks are up to something. I feel it and I know it after seeing their preparations. Mehmet is desperate, we've cut off his supplies and he must take action. He also knows know that he had succeeded in another world and time."

"And that makes him all the more dangerous."

"Yes, it does and he knows if he fails his own court will overthrow him."

"It's too bad that Janie decided to betray us. Her destiny is now tied with him."

"Women fall in love too easy."

"That is why they are dangerous. Cleopatra brought down Mark Anthony."

Suddenly the darkness was lit up by a thunderous ripple of cannon fire. They could hear and feel the huge stone balls crashing into the outer walls. "They are hitting the Saint Stefanos gate."

"That's where they got in during my time line. Julie must have told him."

"They are aiming all their guns there. Hurry let's see what the damage is." They jumped on their horses and galloped towards the wall.

When they reached the Saint Stefanos gate they could see that the outer walls had in fact been seriously breached. Soon they could hear the yells of thousands of men coming across the causeway headed toward the breaches. The guns on the walls began firing towards the general area, but they could not yet see any targets. Visibility was less than then 20 meters. "They will get into the inner walls. We should be able to contain them there."

They were soon joined by General Perdakis and his staff.

"General Notaras, I have called in the reserves. The enemy is pouring through the breach."

They could all hear non-stop rifle fire and the occasional bark from the nine pounders coming from the vicinity of the Saint Stefanos gate. George was also getting reports from several of his Americans via his com gear that the enemy were in very close quarters with the defenders. The breach was bad and the defenders were barely holding their own. With the arrival of the reserves they were able to throw the undisciplined irregular Ottoman infantry back through the breaches. Hundreds of enemy troops lay dead or dying between the walls. For now the attack was over. The Byzantines had held but had also suffered many casualties in the hand to hand fighting, unable to use their weapons superiority, due to the foggy conditions.

"This is not good. The breaches are very large, they will attack again. If they manage to knock down more of the walls we are in real trouble," General Notaras said.

Another ripple of gunfire could be heard coming from the enemy positions. Almost immediately several hits registered on the walls including a large 1000-pound ball, which hit the inner wall knocking down a small section. "Plug that gap. Get some infantry there before they attack us in force," General Perdakis yelled to his senior officers.

From the Turkish lines came the sound of music and cymbals clashing. "Here they come," George said.

Cannon fire erupted between the walls as the Byzantine

gunners let loose trying to stop the hordes of enemy troops that came through the gaps screaming, "Allah Akbar" at the top of their lungs. Several very large explosions erupted between the walls silencing the musket fire. "My god they blew themselves up and took our men with them!" General Notaras said.

"He is using Taliban tactics, suicide Jihadi bombers. Janie must have told him about the Taliban in Afghanistan and he's decided to use the same tactics. They have small barrels filled with gunpowder and bullets strapped to their back with a short fuse."

"Well, we are screwed; they've just taken out a good number of our reserve force."

"We need more men here now! Go get the Imperial Guard."

"There guarding the north walls," General Perdakis shouted.

"It's here, were they're breaking through."

"Yes, sir. I'll send a runner immediately."

Another large explosion caused another section of the inner wall to collapse. "They're planting explosives on the walls. If they continue the attack they will soon be in the city in force."

George called Jenkins and ordered him set up the mortars and prepare both the Humvee and BMP to deploy. George prayed they would hold until the sun came up so they could see better and use their weapons advantage. From their vantage point on the top of the inner wall they could hear the yells of hundreds of enemy soldiers pouring through the gap.

"Sir, ready with the mortar. I am set up about 500 meters from your position."

"Drop one between the walls."

"On the way." A few seconds later the round landed off 50 meters to the left."

"Jenkins, correct 50 meters right."

"On the way, sir."

"On target, fire ten rounds for effect."

It was the turn of the provincial troops to attack. Several of them had sacrificed their lives blowing themselves up to open a way for their comrades to get through. Hundreds were now pouring through the gap. The well placed mortar rounds began to land among the enemy cutting them down like a scythe. By the time the last round had landed over a hundred had been killed and scores wounded. The remainder went to ground amongst the ruble of the outer wall and began pouring arrows, grenades and gunfire at the defenders.

Ottoman Front Lines
13 November 1452

Mehmet watched the attacks from the front lines. Some progress had been made at the costs of thousands of lives. It would be daybreak soon and the advantage would go to the Byzantines because they would be able to use their weapons superiority against him. It was time he sent in the Janissaries, but first there would be another attack of his Taliban volunteers.

Mustafa Pasha, send in the martyrs."

"By your command, my padishah."

It was less than half an hour before daybreak. The Sultan now only had one fresh corps, his own palace regiments which included the Janissaries. He gave the order to march forward.

"Commanders, you will now attack with the Janissaries."

Three thousand men armed with guns, grenades, cross bows and swords advanced with terrifying discipline, moving slowly and with no noise towards the main breach at the Saint Stefanos gate. The sultan accompanied them to the edge of the breach. The fighting went on back and forth for almost 45 minutes before one of the Jihadi bombers on the left flank of the fighting reached the Porta Xelokerko gate and detonated his charge destroying the structure. One of the Janissary commanders on the left saw the opportunity and charged the gate with fifty men. They rushed inside and up the internal stairs case and raised their banner on the battlement. When the Byzantine troops saw the banner, some began to panic yelling the "Turks are behind us."

Both George and General Notaras were watching the disaster unfold before them. "We need to seal that breach and take the wall back or else we are screwed. I will take the men from this section."

"They are not enough."

"We need more men, get the rest of the reserves."

"The Imperial Guard are already committed there are only one hundred left guarding the palace. We should not have sent all those troops to Selybria."

"It's no use crying over spilled milk, general. That's what made him throw everything at us. If we can hold him here he is finished, it's over. "

"If we can't, George, it's over for us."

"Go get the Admiral's marines and use them to plug the breach. I am going to the palace. If we can't hold them I will use the BMP. It's our only hope."

"Go with god my friend and good luck."

"Thank you general. I will need all the luck I can get. George grabbed about thirty men mostly armed with flintlocks and ran towards the breach.

Panic began to spread amongst the defenders spurred by the sight of an Ottoman banner on the wall. Mehmet had been joined by Zaganos Pasha his grand vizier. Both men noticed the confusion of the Byzantine defenders. "We now have an opportunity to take the inner wall. We need more men there to assist and hold, my padishah."

"I see it too." Mehmet called to one of his reserve Janissary commanders a giant of a man named Hassan Ulubad. "Take thirty men and secure the inner wall till reinforcements arrive."

"Yes, my sultan."

Dawn was beginning to break as Hassan and his men ran toward the breach and began climbing the stairs. When they reached the top of the wall Hassan was the first out, only to be cut down by a .556mm round fired by George. Several of Hassan's men were also cut down by accurate musket fire before they took cover. George watched in horror as more banners began to appear on the walls. "Fix bayonets and prepare to charge."

George grabbed one of his few remaining grenades pulled the pin and tossed it towards the area where the remainder of Hassan's men were taking cover. The grenade exploded killing and wounding several of the enemy defenders. "Let's take them out men. For the empire!" He yelled at the top of his lungs.

The Byzantines crashed into the stunned Ottomans like madmen. George kept pulling the trigger until he heard the hammer click on an empty chamber. He quickly pulled out a spare magazine, but the man he tried to shoot, had a primitive gun in his hand and was bringing it up to fire. "Die infidel dog."

Before George could insert the new magazine the Janissary's weapon fired sending a large lead ball towards George, striking him in the chest and knocking him down. Fortunately for George his body amour, designed to stop 21st century high velocity projectiles stopped the low velocity led ball in its tracks. George quickly recovered, got up and shot the offending soldier.

"Say hello to Allah for me." The man died with a puzzled look on his face. It looked for a moment that the Byzantines would retake the wall but several dozen fresh Janissary troops arrived and joined the fray.

"Pull back we can't hold them," George yelled.

The Ottomans now had several hundred troops inside the inner walls. George knew that if something was not done soon it would be almost nearly impossible to dislodge them and the city would be lost. They had retreated to a safer position a couple of hundred yards down the wall, which was covered by two 12 pounder guns. There he met up with General Perdakis and his staff.

"General Mavrakis what is happening? Can we hold them?"

The two guns fired in unison sending explosive shells towards the enemy. "The Turks have breached the walls; we need to hold them in that area, we can't let them advance anymore. We will fight them house to house if necessary and make them pay dearly with blood, for every meter they take. Send runners and pull eight men out of every ten off the walls and bring them here."

"Yes, I too see that the threat is right here in this area. If they widen the breach and advance further south, the city is lost."

"I am going to get the BMP and whatever else I can find to stem their advance and push them back" George took one of the officer's horses and galloped toward the palace. On the way there he noticed 100 Byzantine cavalry men heading towards the breach. They were pulling two nine pounders. He would put his evacuation plan in affect. George used his communication device to have all his American troops meet at the palace immediately.

When George reached the palace, he saw everyone waiting by the BMP and the Humvee including the emperor with a company of Imperial Guards armed with Nagants and flintlock muskets. "Is it time to use this metal monster, General?"

"Yes your majesty. They have breached the walls and have gained a foothold. We must push them back and stop their advance or the city is lost."

"We're ready sir," Captain Jenkins said.

"Men this is it. If we fail to stop them soon, the city will fall. The enemy is going for broke they are throwing everything they have at us. We are barely holding them at the moment. They've made some significant gains and they are slowly advancing along the inner wall despite horrendous casualties."

"We're ready to fight and give them hell, sir."

"I know you are Davis, we all are. Davis you will man the Humvee machine gun. We are low on machine gun ammo so make every bullet count."

"You can depand on that, sir."

"Thompson, you'll be driving the Hummer. Lieutenant Ross you will have the M203 grenade launcher."

"Yes, sir."

"Jenkins you will be manning the main gun. Captain Burns will be driving and Williams will be manning the co axial machine gun. Rhodes will be manning the 30 mm AGS-17 grenade launcher. Thankfully this model had one installed it will come in very handy. Use them sparingly make every shot count."

"Yes, Sir."

"The plan is to throw them back and break their offensive capability. Do not let them mob you and cause you to stop. If that happens you're dead."

"We understand, sir."

"Mary and Anna get in now."

Mary tearfully hugged her husband and gave him a long kiss. "Be careful Constantine. I want our child to have a father."

"I will my love, but how can I be an emperor with no empire?"

"We can build a new one in southern Greece if we must. So come back to me."

"I will. I promise you. Now go with the grace of god and good luck! Give them hell general."

"We will your majesty."

Everyone quickly got on board the armored fighting vehicle (AFV) and the ramp was closed. Burns started the 300hp diesel engine. The 13 ton fighting vehicle with the Byzantine eagles emblazoned on its sides and with a Byzantine flag flying from its top, surged forward in the mostly empty streets. Those people that saw it clanking through the streets crossed them-selves in fear, but also prayed the metal beast would save them from the ravages of the Ottoman hoards, that were sure to come if the city fell. The gunfire and screaming got louder as they neared the fighting. The enemy had managed to push deeper into the immediate area and place more banners on the walls.

"Sir, enemy soldiers at ten o'clock on the walls."

"I see them Leroy. Rhodes give em a few 30mm rounds."

"On the way, sir." The AGS-17, Plamya grenade launcher fired off a few high explosive rounds at the several dozen enemy troops that were running on the wall. The rounds impacted on the stones sending shrapnel in every direction, killing and wounding many of enemy soldiers. The survivors retreated in panic towards the Ottoman bridgehead. When the AFV reached the battle zone, they came in contact with General Notaras who had arrived with reinforcements pulled from other sections of the walls. He had also brought along a few 9 and 12 pounder guns that were already firing shells and solid rounds into buildings that the enemy had seized

"I'm glad you're here with that metal beast. Hopefully we can stem their advance in this sector. We are barely holding here. I fear that they have advanced deeper into the city just north of here."

"We'll do our best, sir." George noticed several enemy soldiers firing at them with crossbows and hand guns from a stone structure less than 100 meters distant. They all heard a scream as one of the cross bow bolts struck a soldier in the shoulder.

George pointed to the structure. Jenkins nodded his head and manually loaded an armor piercing round in the 73 mm 2A28 "Grom" low pressure smoothbore semi-automatic gun. He traversed the turret pointing it towards the stone building and fired. The 73mm round was designed to penetrate the armor of most NATO 1970s main battle tanks, such as the German Leopard 1 and the American M60A1A. The shell easily penetrated the heavy wooden front door, struck the stone wall and exploded blowing the roof off the building and killing most of those inside. The remaining survivors struggled out of the destroyed structure and were cut down by the BMP's PKT 7.62mm machine gun.

"General, I will leave you the Humvee with a machine gun and Ross with the grenade launcher. I am heading north to see what's going on."

"Push them back general before we lose total control of the situation."

"Will do, sir. See you in a bit. Good luck."

Burns put the vehicle in gear and headed north paralleling the wall which was now adorned with enemy banners. Many buildings adjacent to the inner wall were burning, set afire by grenades and cannon shells. They could see scores of Janissaries on and around the walls fighting with swords and axes against Byzantine troops armed with bayonet tipped rifles and swords. The Byzantines were giving ground but were also exacting a high price in blood from the enemy. He could not use the AFV's main armaments for fear of hitting his own troops. "Sir, what are we going to do? The fighting is at close quarter and we'll kill our own guys."

"I can see that. This does not look good. They've advanced pretty far and more troops are pouring in by the minute.

"Sir, this vehicle is amphibious. We can cross into the Galatas straights and come in behind them. I checked all the seals they looked pretty good."

"That's a great idea Jenkins. Let's do it. Burns head for the naval yard."

"Yes, sir."

Several minutes later they went through the gate and into the sprawling naval base. George saw Admiral Laskaris with a company of marines. George had the AFV stopped and he got out. "Where in god's name are you going with that iron beast?"

"Admiral, the enemy has penetrated into the city at two locations. They are being contained at the St Stefano gate, with the Humvee providing fire support, but they have also advanced northwards along the wall. This fighting vehicle can also travel in water. I will take it through the Galatas straits and come out behind them and attack them from the rear."

"That is a brilliant move, George, make it so because we are quickly running out of time."

"You should take the marines about a half mile south and hold the enemy there. The area is very defensible."

"We will do that. Good luck, general."

George got back into the AFV and climbed into the commander's seat. Burns gave it the gas and the vehicle moved forward towards the wharfs. When they reached the docks they could see the remaining warships of the fleet preparing to get underway. If the city fell there was no way that the ships would fall into enemy hands. They would load as many of the surviving troops and citizens that they could and head for southern Greece. The partially completed steam frigate had several sailors standing by to burn it and the facilities, if the enemy entered the naval yards. The same would be done to all the weapons factories. Most of the dyes and casts for the guns had been loaded on naval vessels and would be brought along if they had to evacuate. If the city fell, George would head to the underground base top off his tanks take as many barrels of diesel they could strap on the AFV and Humvees,. They would also load as many fuel barrels as possible on the ships along with other useful equipment and blow the base to hell. He would then head overland towards the Peloponnese, a 1000 mile journey. He would arrange for refueling rendezvous along the way. It would be difficult, but possible. George prayed it would not come to that.

"Here's the water, sir. Let's see if she floats."

"Stay in the shallows as much as possible."

"Aye, aye, captain," Burns said jokingly.

The AFV slowly entered the calm waters of Galatas inlet and

proceeded northwest following the shoreline. "So far so good, sir. We haven't sprung any leaks."

"We're almost there anyway. When we come on shore we will make for the Saint Stefanos gate. You will start shooting when I give the order. The more panic we can create, the better."

"Yes, sir."

"Jenkins, use your ammo wisely. That's all we got. Make every round count."

They had reached the end of the inlet and the AFV slowly climbed onto the shore. They were now about a mile behind the Ottoman siege lines. "Give her the gas and prepare to turn on a smoke screen. That will scare the hell out of them."

"Yes, sir. Here we go!"

"Wait just a minute." George stepped down from the commander's seat and opened the troop carrier. "This is it everybody. We're going for broke."

"Let's give them hell sarge," yelled Mary over the din of the engines making everyone laugh.

"I hear you. God bless the US air force, at least the one 550 years in the future."

George climbed back up to the commander's seat. "Let her rip, Burns."

"Here we go again."

The BMP1 surged ahead at 20 miles an hour, as it neared the enemy lines George gave the order to make smoke. To a 15th century soldier the speeding AFV looked like a demon from hell. No matter what their officers had told their troops about the soldiers and weapons from the future, many still panicked and ran. Others stood their ground and died. The BMP 1 continued its desperate charge, crashing through tents, crushing men and animals that got in the way. The 13 ton AFV roared through the Ottoman lines, spitting out bullets and 30mm grenades, killing and wounding scores as it continued its mad dash.

"Jenkins, take out that giant cannon before it fires."

"On it, sir."

The smoothbore 73mm gun fired once, sending a 73mm high explosive round at the large cannon. The round exploded by the gunners setting off the near-by stored powder. The large explosion sent the huge gun crashing into troops killing dozens. When the AFV neared the wall breaches, several enemy troops charged toward it holding lit bottles in their hands that looked like Molotov cocktails. "What the hell are they carrying, Sir?"

"Whatever it is don't let them get close enough so they can threw it at us."

The men ran towards the AFV but were gunned down, not before one was able to toss his lit bottle at the oncoming behemoth. The bottle hit the front of the vehicle and shattered. Flames engulfed the front end of the AFV as the alcohol and sugar ignited and began to burn. Fortunately, the flaming contents missed the driver position by only a foot.

"That was pretty close, sir.

"It aint over, yet. Here come some more." A group of Janissaries tossed several objects that exploded. Jenkins yelled in pain as a piece of shrapnel hit him in the arm causing a small gash. He fired a burst and gunned down the enemy soldiers.

"Jenkins, are you okay? The bastards are throwing grenades. We may have to button up as we reach the walls."

"Just a small gash, sir. I'll be okay. I won't be able to use the machine gun or grenade launcher if we button up."

"Then be extra careful. George was furious that Janie had

further betrayed them by telling them about Molotov cocktails as a way to destroy the BMP."

The AFV was now at the large wall breach that had been made by the Ottoman cannons. Much of it was obscured by the smoke of burning buildings, set alight by cannon fire and suicide bombers. "If you can make it through, take us inside the inner wall, Burns."

"Yes, sir. It should not be a problem."

"Let them have it as soon as you see targets of opportunity. Just make every shot count."

"With pleasure, sir."

CHAPTER 5

Ottoman Front Lines
13 Nov 1452

Mehmet and his staff observed the progress of the battle. The attack had gone better than planned. Aided by darkness and the thick fog, his gunners had been able to move their artillery to almost point blank range, enabling them to take down large sections of the wall. He thanked Allah that Janie had told him about the Taliban Jihadi suicide bombers, she had faced in Afghanistan. He quickly had his Mufti issue a Fatwa praising Jihad and martyrdom. Thus, when he put the word out looking for martyrs there was no lack of jihadi volunteers. It had been a brilliant move. Not expecting this type of attack, hundreds of defenders had been decimated by the suicide attacks. Before the Byzantine infantry could recover from the Jihadist attacks, his engineers had placed explosives on the inner walls and were able to blow a breach through them. His Janissaries had done the rest. Victory was now within his grasp.

"My padishah, our men have penetrated almost 500 paces into the city and are spreading out. One of our units has reached the outskirts of their naval base. But now we are beginning to meet very stiff resistance."

"They are desperate and throwing everything they have at us. Keep up the pressure. Victory is close at hand. Constantinopolis will fall to us this day. Send in more troops. Use the Sipahi."

"But they are cavalry units my sultan."

"I know what they are you fool. But if they are able to get into the city and behind their lines, they will cause panic and take vital troops from the frontlines to chase them down."

"Yes my padishah. I will immediately carry out your orders."

Mehmet wished he had more free thinking commanders that would take the initiative, instead of him having to tell the idiots what to do.

Suddenly the sound of rapid explosions and machinegun fire coming from the area of the Saint Stefanos gate sent a shiver through his spine. He screamed at one of his commanders to bring his company of Janissaries along. Mehmet ran towards the breach and saw a huge steel monster coming through the opening spitting out death to all those that approached it.

Mehmet saw victory slipping through his fingers. This iron monster was virtually unstoppable unless his men were able to hit it with fire bombs. Unfortunately no one was able to get close enough. All those that attempted it were cut down by its machine gun. To make matters even worse, the Byzantines forces began counterattacking once the saw they saw the BMP.

"In the name of Allah, death to the infidels! Light your bombs and destroy this satanic machine. I will give 10000 gold to the man that burns it." Mehmet yelled in frustration.

The sultan watched as several men lit their fire bombs and ran towards the metal monster, but they were unable to get close enough to throw their bombs, being cut down by a hail of bullets. Now that the fog had finally cleared, the Byzantine infantry began using their superior weaponry. He watched as several of their smaller cannon began spitting out death, cutting down dozens of his men with canister rounds as they tried to advance.

Byzantine rifleman also began exacting a heavy toll on the attackers.

"My padishah, we must pull back the Byzantine naval soldiers are attacking from our right and they will soon outflank us."

Mehmet looked at his grand vizier. "Is there any way my friend that we can save this situation? We have come so close and paid such a heavy price to have victory snatched from us."

"No my padishah. We can't hope to stop that infernal machine of death that is massacring our men."

Mehmet watched as the iron monster kept advancing and dishing out mayhem and death to his troops. "You are right my friend we must put our plan in effect and evacuate to Anatolia. This battle is lost. It's a miracle that our men have not yet broken and ran. It is only a matter of time before they do."

"I have made the arrangements, my padishah; we must leave as soon as possible before your commanders can act against you."

"I must return and get Janie. She is very valuable to us."

"And you have a spot in your heart for her."

"Yes that is true. Let's try and save as many men as we can. Give the orders to retreat and I will meet you back at my tent."

"Hurry my padishah, this retreat will soon become a rout once the Byzantines get organized and counter attack in force, which they will

"They have very competent commanders," Mehmet replied thinking of the American general.

Just as he was about to leave a dispatch rider arrived. He got off his horse and prostrated himself in front of the sultan. "Get up man what is your message?"

"My sultan the Venetian fleet has been sighted they will be

arriving within the hour."

"Now it is really over," said the grand vizier. "Go as planned, my padishah. I will be right behind you."

The sultan jumped on his white stallion and headed back toward his encampment, followed by his Janissary body guards. When he reached his tent he found Janie who was dressed in her combat gear, his Janissary commander and his brother-in-law waiting for him. "Mehmet what happened?"

"We were winning. Our men were inside the city pushing the enemy back. Then they attacked us from the rear with that satanic metal monster."

"I thought you said fire bombs can destroy it?" The Janissary general, said.

"It's unstoppable our men could not get close enough to throw their fire bombs. Anyone that tried died in his tracks. Our attack has been repulsed and the Byzantines are counter attacking. We must leave at once for Anatolia."

"I am with you my brother."

"My life is in your hands now, Ismail Bey. If we can make it to Anatolia we can live and fight another day."

"Let's get out of here before the infidel's iron monster arrives and kills us all."

"Yes, we must leave immediately. As soon as my chests are loaded on the horses we go."

Within 30 minutes everything was loaded and with 500 janissaries and a company of Sipahi, they set off toward the town of Stenia on the Bosporus, a ten mile journey. Hopefully they would find the boats that were waiting for them to cross into Anatolia.

Constantinopolis
13 November 1452

The Ottoman attack had quickly stalled once the AFV had reached the inner walls and began engaging the enemy troops there. Several of the enemy soldiers had tried to toss Molotov's, but thanks to Captain Jenkins' accurate machine gun and grenade fire were never able to get close enough to be successful. When the Marines under Admiral Laskaris' command finally counter attacked, they were quickly joined by the Imperial Guard regiment under the emperor's command. The Ottoman Janissaries bravely tried to hold their ground, but they died under accurate rifle fire or the bayonets of the guard. Eventually unable to advance or retreat many threw down their arms and surrendered, while many others broke and fled in panic. At first the Ottoman retreat had been orderly but seeing the Janissaries flee in panic, the rest of the troops dropped their weapons and ran for their lives. This resulted in a complete route for the rest of the Ottoman forces.

George spotted the emperor who was on foot, armed with an AK47 assault rifle and ordered the AFV to stop. He got out of the commander's seat and went up and saluted his commander and chief. "We did it your majesty. We beat them."

"Yes my friend, but at a very heavy cost, thousands gave their lives today. It was a very close thing. But we have broken the back of their attack and we must continue the destruction of their army. They will either surrender or die. They will have no other option."

"Yes your majesty. I still have the empress with me."

"Keep her for the time being, she is safer with you. There are still many of the enemy loose in the city. It will be a while till they are all killed or captured."

"I will keep her safe, Anna is also with her."

"I also just received a report that the Venetian fleet has been sited and will be here very soon."

"So it seems our Italian friends kept their word."

"Seems so general, but they were a bit late."

"Best for them to have us at a weakened state, fortunately that is not the case. We have been damaged pretty bad but not totally weakened."

"Thank god, we still have a powerful navy."

"I would still keep our gun batteries manned and pointing towards the sea. Better be safe than sorry."

"Good advice my friend. I will ensure we do that. We don't want a repeat of the 4th crusade. Now let's finish what the Ottomans started."

"I will do just that, Constantine. Now be careful and secure the city. I would post artillery and the Humvee at the wall breaches until they are repaired. We don't want any surprises."

"Your advice has been noted my friend. We will be mopping up behind you."

George saluted and jumped back into the AFV. "Burns take us through the enemy lines and head towards the sultan's camp."

Burns gunned the engine and headed towards the sultan's encampment. When the Ottoman troops saw the AFV, most dropped their weapons and ran away or raised their hands. Those that resisted died on the spot. When they reached the area where the sultan's tents were, they found it deserted. George stopped the AFV and got out, "Jenkins I'll check the tents you keep your finger near the trigger for any hostiles."

"I will sir. Please be very careful. We can't afford to have anything happen to you at this stage."

George took his assault rifle with him and cleared all the nearby tents. "They're all empty, looks like they made a quick getaway."

"I wonder which way they're headed, sir?"

"I don't know, but here come the friendlies. A couple of minutes later they were joined by a company of Byzantine cavalry. Their commander, a major, dismounted his horse went over to George and saluted.

"Sir, the enemy is surrendering in droves; we have captured many thousands of prisoners. Those that refuse to surrender are killed on the spot."

"Are many refusing to surrender, major?"

"No sir. Most surrender and throw themselves to our mercy."

"A very wise choice at this point."

"I wonder if any of the prisoners know where the sultan went."

"I am sure we can find out for you sir. Give us a few minutes."

The major jumped on his horse and galloped off. Ten minutes later he returned with an Ottoman officer. "Sir, this man said that the sultan had taken off with several hundred Janissaries and cavalry towards the east."

"Thank you, major. Please make sure this man is not harmed."

"Yes, sir."

George jumped back into the commander's seat. "Okay everybody back into the vehicle we got a sultan to catch."

10 Miles east of Constantinopolis
13 Nov 1452

After leaving his encampment, the sultan and his escort travelled east toward the small seaside town of Stenia. It was almost sun set when they finally reached the outskirts. There he was joined by his grand vizier, who had ridden ahead after leaving the battlefield, to ensure the arrangements he had made were being kept. The sultan dismounted his horse and walked up to his grand vizier. "So is everything in order?"

"Yes, my padishah. There are 20 boats in the harbor waiting to ferry us across the Bosporus. Each captain expects five pieces of gold for every trip."

"I am fine with that."

"Let's get moving before any enemy cavalry units or ships arrive and attempt to stop us."

Before Mehmet could reply, he heard the Janissary commander screaming at him. He turned towards the man and saw that he was pointing a fire arm at him. "You are a coward Mehmet and not fit to lead the Ottoman tribes any longer. You led us to defeat and now you are trying to escape to save your hide. You are not fit to be sultan."

Before the sultan could pull the Beretta pistol Janie had given him, the Janissary officer squeezed the trigger shooting Mehmet in lower right side. Before he collapsed, he was able to fire a shot killing the man. Janie grabbed her assault rifle and pointed it towards the other Janissary officers. "If any man tries anything they will die."

She rushed over to the fallen sultan and pulled out her combat first aid kit. She looked at the wound; it was serious and would require medical attention. She put some antiseptic powder on it and applied a pressure bandage to stem the bleeding.

She gave her weapon to the grand vizier. "Here take my weapon. All you do is point it and squeeze the trigger."

"How is he," the grand vizier asked.

"He's passed out. The wound is bad. He needs a physician."

"We will get him one, when we reach the other side."

"I don't know if he will live that long, the shock and movement may kill him."

"We don't have a choice, if we stay here his own men or the enemy may kill him."

Mehmet started to shake his head and awaken; Janie could see the pain from the wound reflected on his face. "Don't move Mehmet, you have been wounded."

"We can't stay here, the enemy will catch us or my own men will murder us. Leave me and go back to your friends."

"No, I won't leave you. I am a traitor to them now."

"Where is my grand vizier?"

"I am here, my padishah."

"Take her back to the other Americans. They won't harm her."

They heard the roar of a vehicle approaching. "It's too late, the iron monster has arrived."

"Tell the men to drop their arms and raise their hands. No more men need to die because of me. It's over. I will be with the prophet very soon."

The grand vizier and the surviving janissary officers spread the word to their men. When the AFV arrived, the janissaries were lined up and had their hands in the air in surrender. The AFV stopped and a man got out. Janie ran up to him. "Where is the sultan, Janie?

"He was shot by one of his own senior commanders. He will die if he does not get medical attention."

"Take me to him."

George followed her to a small clearing where several men were holding torches over a body on the ground. Burns pulled up with the AFV and shined the vehicle headlights at the group watching over the sultan. Jenkins had the machine gun also trained on them in case someone decided to do something stupid. The young sultan looked up at George. "Well general, it seems you have won after all. But I did come very close in defeating you. It now seems I will never be known in history as Mehmet the conqueror after all. Maybe they will call me Mehmet the failure."

"You did come very close. Many men have died on both sides. This war is now over."

"Yes it is. I intended it to be over. I was fleeing to Anatolia to stay with my brother-in-law. But it now seems I won't make it. Please take Janie with you. She will be killed by my own men or worse if she stays."

George stared at the young man for a moment lying there.

"You're not dead yet. I'll be right back."

George walked over to the AFV and opened the back ramp.

"Anna your medical services are needed." She grabbed her bag and walked over to where the sultan was lying.

"Anna!" Janie ran over and hugged her. "Please help him? He's hurt pretty bad and has lost lots of blood."

"I will do my best, Janie."

She went over and began examining the wounded young sultan. "So you are the beautiful miracle doctor? Janie has told me much about you."

"So you are the young man responsible for the deaths of thousands?"

"Yes, that is me, but it was war and in war many die."

"Stop talking, you will need your strength."

A few minutes later she stood up. "Can you help him please?" The grand vizier asked."

"He's been gut shot and has lost a lot of blood. I don't know what damage the bullet has done, unless I go in and get it out."

"Will he die?"

"If that bullet does not come out and the damage is too great, yes, he will die."

Janie began to cry. "Please help him."

"I don't have the facilities here. We can't move him to far he will bleed to death."

"Then do what you can, please, Anna."

"Pick him up and bring him to the vehicle."

Several of the janissaries came over and lifted the sultan and put him in a crudely made stretcher. They lifted him up and moved him to the back of the AFV. "Okay everyone out." The AFV had a folding table in the compartment which they pulled out and laid the sultan on it, causing him to groan in pain.

"I will also need some hot water to clean up."

"Mary, you are here too. I'm glad to see you."

"I wish I could say the say the same for you, after you sold us out to your new boyfriend."

"I'm so sorry, but I love him. He had no super weapons to fight with and you still defeated him."

"It was a very close thing and thousands have died."

"Janie, come over here and give me a hand with him."

Janie held Mehmet's hand as Anna prepped him for surgery.

"I can't believe you are helping me after all that has happened."

"I am a doctor Mehmet, it's my job and duty to help all those in need, no matter who they are and what they have done. It's also in our military code that we help even our enemies once they have been wounded."

"Well, I thank you."

"Don't thank me yet, you may not survive the surgery."

"Regardless, I will be dead if you don't try."

Anna looked up from a blood test that she had just done.

"We have another problem. He has a rare blood type, AB negative. I doubt he will survive without a blood transfusion."

"I have the same blood type," Janie said.

"You are very lucky Mehmet that Janie has the same blood type as you. Once I have the transfusion set up, you will receive some of her blood to replace what you have lost and will lose during the surgery. Without her blood you will surely die."

"Now besides my heart I owe her my life. Her blood will also flow in my veins."

"I will put you to sleep now and I will start the operation."

While the surgery went on, George sat alone by one of the adjacent campfires thinking of what to do with his prisoner. He could take him back to the city and demand a hefty ransom for his release, but he doubted the Ottoman nobility or military would pay anything, especially if they already tried to kill him. George heard footsteps and saw the Grand Vizier approaching. He was holding two cups and offered one to George.

"Nothing like a cup of hot Tsai (tea) to ward off the night chill."

"Thank you." George took a sip of the hot aromatic beverage.

"Yes it does ward off the chill."

"What were you thinking, General Mavrakis? Were you contemplating our fate?"

"Yes, in fact I was. I don't know what to do with you. At this point your hides aren't worth very much for ransom, to the Ottoman nobility. They may though pay us just to take you back and execute you."

"That is indeed very possible. But if the sultan dies, it really won't matter. My value is only what the sultan deems its worth. Without him I am worthless."

"That is a very good point you make, Zaganos Pasha."

"I am a practical man."

"So am I. If anyone can save your sultan it's my wife. She is the best skilled surgeon on this entire world. She still has some modern medicines with her and with Janie's blood, he has a fighting chance."

"That is good to hear. He is very enamored with the young lady, almost to the point of foolishness."

"It's called love."

"It was very strange. When she was first brought in he had her stripped and flogged, to break her. She talked, but she also fell in love with him. They both did. She bewitched him."

"Love works in strange ways."

"Yes it does. If he survives, he will be your best bet to make peace with the Ottomans, especially if she remains by his side as his wife and advisor."

"Is he not already married?"

"Ottoman sultans have many wives. From what I see she will be his number one wife."

"Knowing Janie, she will be his only wife." Both men laughed out loud.

"Think about it general. The Ottoman nobility will want revenge for their defeat. They will gather a larger army and attack you again and again till they wear you down."

"So what do you propose?"

"A treaty if the young sultan survives the night. Let us cross into Anatolia and we will stay on that side of the straights."

"I am going to take Andrianoupolis (Edirne) your capital and chase you out of Europe anyway."

"Let us have Asia and some of the Levant (Middle East) and you can have the Aegean coast up to 100 miles inland and all of the Balkans."

"You also have done great damage to the city. We will demand 100,000 in gold and a tribute of 50,000 gold pieces for 3 years and free trade. We also want an embassy in your new capital."

"Agreed, we will send diplomats to discuss the fine points. I may even come to participate in the discussions. This is all pending, that we reach our new capital of Konya safely."

"Of course I understand. Excuse me I must go back to my vehicle and brief the emperor on what we just discussed."

"How will you do this?"

"There is a machine there called a radio. With that we can talk over long distances to another radio that is located in the city."

"In the name of Allah the merciful, will these surprises ever cease?"

"Be ready for many more, my friend." George walked over to the AFV contacted headquarters and briefed the emperor on the proposed agreement. It took a bit of convincing, but he too agreed, wishing to avoid an ongoing war with the Ottomans for now. The emperor would send the remaining Humvee to pick up his wife and also deliver a copy of the proposed treaty.

Both men talked until the sun came up, finally Anna appeared with Janie. Both women looked exhausted. "How did it go?" George asked.

"Well, I removed the bullet. Fortunately for him it missed most of his intestines. One was slightly nicked but I managed to clean out the wound and repair the damage. I gave him some penicillin to ward off any infection."

"Will he live?" The grand vizier asked.

"He is young and strong. I think he will make it to live to a ripe old age."

"Thank you, doctor. We both owe you and your husband a great debt we can never repay."

"You can start by ending this war."

"We have already done that with your husband."

"That is a good start. My patient now needs lots of rest and you must ensure the wound is kept clean and bandages are changed regularly to avoid infection. I gave some spares to Janie."

"Is the sultan awake?"

"Yes he is but he needs rest?"

"I must advise him of our agreement."

"Okay, make it quick."

Twenty minutes later, a smiling Zaganos Pasha emerged from the AFV. "He is asleep. He agrees to everything and wishes to convey his thanks and the great debt owed to both of you. We would not have been as generous to a defeated enemy."

"Being generous to a defeated enemy can sometimes ensure a lasting peace. We have done this many times throughout our history. Janie can tell you more about it."

"Yes, we have much to learn. We must now cross the straights and get to Anatolia to begin our long journey."

"Will you be safe on the other side?"

"I believe so. Mehmet's brother-in laws army is there. There are at least 15000 troops to ensure the sultan's safety."

A steam whistle pierced the early morning "There is your

ride. The Niki will take you, the sultan and your horses to the other side."

"Thank you my friend I was never expecting that."

The AFV carried the injured sultan to the dock, where the Niki and several galleys were waiting to transport the sultan and his entourage to the other side. The BMP stopped at the dock and the sultan was carried off the AFV in a stretcher. Before he was carried onto the Niki he wanted a word with George. He held out his hand to George. George took it, "thank you again general for your generous terms to a vanquished foe. I will take care of Janie. Her blood is now in me. I live because of her."

"Just keep your word, Mehmet and we will keep ours."

"Just one more request."

"What is that?"

"Don't let any of my troops cross the straight for at least seven days. I don't need any assassins coming after me in the state I am in."

"Okay, it a deal."

The sultan smiled and waved goodbye as he was carried on to the Niki by his body guards.

Chapter 6

Andrianoupolis (Edirne)
10 January 1453

The great siege had been over for a several weeks. The Byzantine victory against the Ottomans had been total; they had captured almost 40000 prisoners, huge amounts of supplies and over 150,000 pieces of gold. The Ottoman ability to wage war had been neutralized for a long time. The Orthodox prelate sent his priest among the prisoners to spread the word of Jesus. Over half of the prisoners choose to convert to Christianity and settle in or around the city with their families. Some even chose to join the Byzantine army. The rest would be allowed to remain in the Byzantine lands to work and farm if they pledged loyalty to the Byzantine crown. Many of them chose that option. The remainder crossed the straights into Ottoman territory.

The Venetian fleet had arrived just as the Ottomans were surrendering, thus their assistance had not been needed leaving the Byzantines in a better negotiating position for future trade and territorial concessions, such as the future status of the island of Crete. The Venetian admiral had been taken on a tour of the fleet steamship and was shown the new frigate. He had even been given a ride on the BMP, thus leaving him with no doubt on the military strength and capabilities of the newly reborn Byzantine state.

With the lifting of the siege, much had to be done to get the city back in order. The walls were quickly rebuilt to more modern standards, to be able to better withstand artillery. Everyone though knew the age of walled cities was now over. Those that did not yet grasp this would pay a heavy price in the future. The modernization of the Byzantine military continued unabated, under the auspices of General Mavrakis and his staff.

A few weeks later, George found himself leading a force of 8,000 men against the old Ottoman capital of Andrianoupolis. He had been joined by Colonel Longo and his contingent, which after the siege everyone to a man had volunteered to join the Byzantine army. The capture of Andrianoupolis was the final obstacle remaining before Constantinoplis and the rest of the empire were connected with a land route to Greece and to the rest of the Balkans and Europe.

George had issued an ultimatum for the city to surrender but the Ottoman defenders refused. "Well my friend it seems the Turk wants to fight."

"I hate to lose lives. We will shell them for a while and see what they decide."

"Yes, that may be the less bloody choice, colonel. Signal the gun batteries to open fire. I want one battery hitting the wall."

"Yes, sir."

A few seconds later the 18 pounder guns opened fire sending explosive shells into the city. Within an hour a significant breach had been made in the wall and smoke could be seen coming from inside the city. "Cease fire!"

"It seems general, that city walls can't withstand modern cannon fire."

"Not the way these were built, colonel. It will require new architecture to design and build forts that will be able to somewhat withstand limited artillery fire."

"I will send them another ultimatum to surrender, sir."

"Give them thirty minutes to decide."

The Byzantine emissary was sent to the walls and gave the ultimatum to surrender, but was fired on and barely escaped with his life. "I guess we got our answer," Colonel Longo said.

"I have an idea. We don't need to waste lives on both sides. Be prepared to charge through the breach when I give the signal."

"What will the signal be?"

"When you hear the AFV firing, that's the signal to move."

George had a gun hitched to the back of the BMP 1 and towed it to about 400 meters from the city gate. The cannon was loaded with round shot and fired at the gate splintering a section of it. "Give it one more shot."

The 18 pounder was quickly reloaded and fired once more. Splinters flew in all directions from the gate. George was standing in the AFV commander's seat. "That should be enough to soften it up. Button up. Jenkins put a HE round through the gate."

"On the way, sir."

The 73mm gun on the AFV turret fired, sending a high explosive round at the structure. The explosion took down what the cannons had left standing. "Take us through Burns, just be careful."

Hearing the explosion, Colonel Longo ordered the guns to fire a few rounds at the breach as he urged his troops forward with fixed bayonets gleaming in the morning sunlight.

Burns gunned the engine and the 13 ton AFV surged forward. It crashed through what was left of the gate and entered the city. Jenkins let loose with controlled bursts with the coaxial machine gun, cutting down scores of enemy infantry. The defenders were soon running in panic and dropping their weapons. They soon reached the area where the walls had been breached by the cannon fire. Seeing the AFV behind them and the Byzantine army coming through the breach, the defenders began surrendering in droves.

"They've had enough, sir."

"It's finally over for now, Jenkins."

"For now, sir?"

"There are many states that will be very envious of us. Especially, our friends, the Venetians. We will be competing with them in the Aegean and the Balkans."

"They are supposed to be our allies. They even returned some holy relics that werestolen in the fourth crusade."

"They are our allies in name and as long as it suits them. In the 15th-16th century, Venice was a powerful city state, having a large mercantile business empire that spanned the Balkans and the Aegean. We will be in direct competition with them. As long as we are powerful, they will leave us alone. In this century, power rules. Besides they received a ship load of drugs and other eqipment."

"We will need allies, sir."

"Yes we will. That is why I want good will between us and the new Ottoman state. Just before we left the city we received a messenger notifying us that the grand vizier will be arriving shortly, to finalize the peace treaty."

"I wonder how Janie is doing."

"I'm sure we will find out. Now let's mop up here. We were lucky they gave up and casualties were light. I will offer them decent terms and they can get on with their lives as loyal subjects to the Byzantine state."

"There moral is broken, sir. After we defeated their main army they knew they did not stand a chance against us. This was just a token resistance to save face."

"Never the less it still cost lives on both sides."

George got out of the vehicle and walked up to Longo. "We did it my friend. It's finally over; the Ottoman grip on Europe has finally been broken!"

"Yes, we did general, thanks to you. It has cost us very much in blood and treasure to achieve."

"You have contributed greatly to this victory. I hope you decide to stay with us permanently, colonel. "

"I will seriously think about it. Maybe I will join my men."

"I hope you do. Now let's get this over with.

Both men followed by two dozen AK47 armed Imperial Guards, marched into what had been the sultan's palace, to find the imposter that had been crowned sultan in Mehmet's place, after the defeat of the Ottoman armies. A short obese middle aged man held by two Imperial Guards was thrown at George's feet. Another older man dressed in Ottoman garb that served as the grand vizier was also present.

The man that held the title of sultan was trembling with fear.

"Stand him up."

The guards picked him up. "I am at your service my lord," the fat man said.

"You have been totally defeated. You are an imposter to the Ottoman thrown. The Byzantine Empire only recognizes Sultan Mehmet as the legitimate Ottoman ruler. Thus you are a traitor to the Ottoman state. You will be handed over to the sultan's representatives and they can do whatever they want with you."

"Please don't give me to my cousin. He will have me killed."

George turned to the older man that served as grand vizier.

"What is your name, sir?"

"Osman Davoutoglu, your excellency."

"Osman, I have been told you are a wise and honest man. I am offering you the position of governor of this city if you pledge your loyalty to Emperor Constantine and the Byzantine state. The inhabitants of this city will have the option to convert to Christianity if they so desire it and the remainder must pledge their loyalty to the emperor and to the state. Everyone will have the freedom to worship whatever religion they wish."

"Are these your only demands on a defeated enemy?"

"Yes, they are. I will leave a thousand men to garrison the city and also leave you a dozen administrators to help you put the city back in order. How much gold to you have?"

"The Ottoman treasury has 200,000 pieces of gold at present."

"We will take 100,000 back to Constantinopolis to add to the Byzantine treasury and the rest will remain here to run the city."

The man was shocked at George's generosity. "What do you say Osman? Will you join us?"

"I accept your most generous offer and I do pledge my loyalty to the emperor and to the empire."

"Thank you, "governor". We will now assist you in putting the new administration in working order and I will return to the capital."

Constantinopolis
14 February 1453

Both the emperor and his senior staff anxiously awaited in the large throne room the arrival of the Ottoman emissaries to begin negotiating the peace treaty between the two states. The guards had already notified them that the Ottoman's had arrived at the city gates. There former enemies would see a new and vibrant Byzantine capital, that now ruled from the Bosporus, to the borders of Serbia and to the southern Peloponnese. It would soon add most of the cost of Asia Minor.

Many of the scars of the siege were still visible. New buildings were going up to replace those that had been destroyed or damaged. Earthen berms were being built in front of the main walls to help dampen the effects of cannon fire. Everyone with any military experience knew that the age of walled cities was over. A new star shaped fortress which would resist artillery fire was being built. The new fort named Saint George, in honor of General George Mavrakis, would defend the approaches to the city. George had shown the Byzantine engineers concrete reinforcement techniques, which they quickly adopted in building the new fortifications. It would mount 24 pounders and the new 32 pounder guns that were being designed in the new gun foundry that had been built after the siege.

One of the Imperial Guards came in and announced the Ottomans arrival at the palace. "This is it your majesty. We will now be discussing our co-existence with the Ottomans."

"Yes general, thanks again to you and your people this city is still in Christian hands and we will now be negotiating from a position of strength."

"We must though use our position of strength very wisely and not punish the loser too hard, that we plant the seeds for a future war of revenge. This was done to the losers of our first great world war. They had to pay enormous sums until bankrupted and had their colonies taken away and divided amongst the winners. Twenty years later, our second world war broke out amongst the same powers. That war cost over 50 million lives and left Europe divided and in ruins."

"We will be stern with them but also act with fairness and with wisdom."

The large doors to the throne room were opened and the officer in charge of the guards announced the arrival of the Ottoman delegation. George recognized the Grand Vizier, Zaganos Pasha, who walked in with several advisers and men carrying chests, but was shocked to see Janie at the rear of the delegation.

The grand vizier walked up to the emperor who was on his throne with the empress sitting by his side and bowed. "Allow me to convey greetings from my sultan your majesty. He wishes you and the empress good health and many healthy children."

"I wish the same for him and good relations between our two nations."

"He also wishes the same your majesty, that is why we are here and my sultan has also sent his wife to convey the seriousness of these negotiations."

"I see that," Constantine said as he glanced at Janie remembering her betrayal that cost so many additional lives and almost resulted in the city falling to the Ottomans.

"I know you don't trust me your majesty but I am here to ensure fairness and have you hear our proposals. We have also brought you 100,000 pieces of gold for war reparations as promised."

"I see that you have gone to the heights of power very fast, but if your husband trusts you judgement then I am fine with that. Let us go into our meeting chambers, but's first let's have some food and refreshments."

"Yes that would be very good," the grand vizier said.

"Please follow us all to the dining room."

They were all seated around a large table, Mary chose to sit with Janie whom she still considered a friend and carried out a conversation about her new life. The lunch consisted of cheeseburgers, which the emperor had acquired a taste for. The Ottomans also seemed to enjoy the American cuisine from the future. When lunch was finally finished, the negotiators retired to the meeting room to discuss the new treaty. The emperor was first to speak. He stood up from his seat and began his opening speech.

"Ladies and gentlemen, after a bloody and destructive war caused by the Ottomans, we are finally here to discuss a treaty of peace and cooperation between our two states. During the bloody struggle, Byzantium emerged victorious, totally crushing its foe in battle. The defeated enemy threw themselves at our feet. We chose to show mercy, and even saved the life of the man who started this war. Would our former enemy have shown us mercy? Or would my head be rotting on a pike up on the city walls for all to see? Would our houses of worship have been desecrated and turned to animal stalls or mosques?" Constantine paused for a moment and stared at the grand vizier and Janie. "We even let our former enemy leave to establish a new kingdom where he could rearm and theoretically threaten us in the future. We hope that the mercy and assistance we gave to our former enemies will bear fruit and develop into a meaningful friendship." The emperor then took his seat.

The grand vizier stood up and began to speak. "Your majesty, you are correct. We would have never shown you any mercy had we taken the city. It would have been pillaged for three days as is our custom and you and your generals would have been killed. By the will of Allah, we lost and you did show us mercy and saved the sultan's life when he had been seriously wounded by one of his own commanders. We are all greatly in your debt, especially the sultan. He has been greatly humbled by your acts of generosity and mercy towards a totally defeated foe. We do wish to live in peace. We will honor our part of the treaty as promised. Ottoman forces will immediately begin pulling back 100 miles from the coast of Asia Minor as we agreed. We will control the port of Seleucia which we will rename Mersin. It will be a naval base and a merchant port. We propose that any new Ottoman acquisitions will be towards the east and middle east-Persian Gulf. We will not interfere with Byzantine acquisitions in the Balkans or the Aegean Sea. These are our proposals."

"At least you are honest, sir, "said the emperor. "This is a good point to start our negotiations. We will expect the Ottoman forces to pull back from the coast in 90 days after the treaty is signed. We will agree on the Ottoman control of the port of Seleucia. To show our good intentions, we will offer you the port of Sinope on the Black sea for trading purposes. We also agree that you can expand eastward. We do have issues with the holy land, but we are all getting ahead of ourselves. The Ottoman military is in no position to take on the Mamelukes at this time. I also suggest we set up a council to discuss and resolve any future disputes peacefully."

"That is a good idea, your majesty. I will mention it to my sultan."

George glanced at the emperor who gave him a nod to speak. "There are many enemies out there in this world who would love to destroy both our nations. They will be envious of our trade and riches. History shows us that having an empire is just not conquering territory and subjugating peoples. You must build infrastructure, schools, and universities and develop a viable economy and technological base."

Janie stood up and interrupted George. "General Mavrakis, my husband is aware of all this. I have given him an excellent history lesson on the future. He is presently consolidating his rule. We know there are many enemies around us, even amongst our own people. My husband also thanks you for turning over the imposter to the Ottoman throne. He will not make the same mistakes other Ottoman rulers made in our time line. We do want to live in peace with you. We do want trade and business and I thank the emperor for his generosity of offering us the port of Sinope for trade purposes. We also understand the importance of education, technology and building infrastructure. My husband at this very moment is establishing the University of Konya and a military academy in our capital. We will invite the best teachers of the world to come and teach and do research at our new facilities. Christians are always welcome to live in our territories and will have the religious freedom to worship as they please. When we all arrived here over a year ago, we changed future history forever. This is an opportunity to make it right and avoid many of the bloody wars we fought against each other."

"Those are very good words, but time will show if they are real. We pray that they are sincere. We hope war between our two states will never happen again. Unfortunately, this city sits on the crossroads of Asia and Europe. It has through the centuries been attacked numerous times by invading armies that want to go east or west."

"You are correct, your majesty. The Ottoman Empire will expand in different directions. We will avoid Europe at all costs. We may even explore and establish colonies elsewhere. We are also willing to sign a non-aggression treaty with you and possibly in the very near future ask for a treaty of alliance, which will prove beneficial to both parties. This is one of the reasons I am here. My husband wanted you to hear this from my lips."

That last statement brought a hush to the table. "That is a very interesting proposal. That's something we will seriously consider. I too received many lectures on the future from my wife and General Mavrakis. I know we will need loyal friends and allies to survive in this new world. As you would say my dear lady, the genie is out of the bottle. Your arrival in this century has speeded up military weapons evolution by hundreds of years. We already have steam power and we will shortly launch our new steam frigate, the Empress Mary, which will be able to cross the Atlantic Ocean and another is already under construction. Even though this technology is secret, other nations will soon copy it. We must all be prepared for this, so we will seriously consider your proposal. We border each other and it behooves us to be friends and yes, maybe even allies. Time will tell. We may even offer you technology. But that is in the future and depended on your future actions."

The grand vizier looked at Janie and spoke. "Thank you your majesty for even considering our proposal. I hope our future actions will prove our sincerity and help build a climate of trust between our two nations. We hope with the signing of this treaty to establish an embassy and a trade mission with you."

"That is a reasonable request. We hope we can send our ambassador and a trade delegation with you and also establish an embassy in your new capital."

"Why of course, we would be most honored to have them return with us to our capital."

"Excellent! I believe we now have a base to focus our discussions and quickly wrap up a treaty."

"Yes, your majesty I believe we do."

Konya (Ikonio), New Ottoman capital
1 March 1453

Sultan Mehmet II and his head wife soon to be his only wife Janie, were enjoying a private dinner together to celebrate the new treaty between the Ottomans and Byzantines. Considering that the Byzantines held all the cards and could if they wanted, quickly roll over his armies. Instead they choose to show restraint and generosity towards a defeated foe. He was sure General Mavrakis had a lot to do with that, but the emperor would still have to approve. They had even given him a trading port on the black sea. He would have never done that. There was a lot he could learn from them as a ruler and diplomat. According to his grand vizier, his wife was a wise negotiator and diplomat. She was able to lower the remaining reparations payments to 25000 gold pieces a year instead of 50000. The savings would help build roads, schools and hospitals. Most of all she had gotten a commitment from the emperor that he would consider an alliance. That would prove valuable since what remained of his empire was surrounded by enemies, the Persians in the east and Mamelukes in the south.

Mehmet looked fondly at his new wife; she was dressed in a two piece Ottoman outfit that accented her sensual figure. She was both beautiful and wise. She had saved his life and his empire. "This is a great day for us my love. We have secured a fair peace on our northern frontier, thanks to you and my grand vizier."

"I think we owe a lot of the generous terms to General Mavrakis, who helped influence Constantine."

"You are right my love. I do owe a great debt to that man. I also owe my life and my throne to him and his wife. Hopefully one day I can repay it."

"You also owe your future son or daughter to him, Mehmet."

"My love, are you with child?"

"Yes, I am pregnant."

Mehmet hugged and kissed her. "That is the best news I have had in months. Allah works in mysterious ways. A union between the past and future. If he is a son he will be indeed a wise sultan with his mother as his tutor and if a daughter, she will be beautiful and smart like her mother, who will one day marry a prince."

"You are so sweet Mehmet. But first we must survive long enough to see that day in a now very unpredictable and unstable world."

"I have become a different person, since I met you my love. I am calmer and I do not make rash decisions. We will survive and prosper. Especially with the new military and economic reforms and the opening of centers of learning that will bring many benefits to our people. The Ottoman Empire will not be the empire of your past timeline. We will adopt with the times and push the cutting edge of technology. I even plan to expand across the Atlantic. Together we will succeed my love. Especially if the Byzantines accept our offer of alliance. Now let's celebrate."

Constantinopolis
17 September 1453

George and Anna held their crying four-month-old daughter as the Orthodox Patriarch Athanasius II gave his final blessings and finished the baptismal service, which was held in front of hundreds of guests in Aghia Sofia cathedral. Next to them stood the child's god father, Emperor Constantine and the godmother Empress Mary. He had baptized her and given her the name Irene (Peace). The emperor turned to George. "I' m glad this is over. I am roasting in here."

"So am I."

"We're baptizing our son in three weeks."

"I know, Anna told me I'll be there."

"I'm sure you will since Anna will be the godmother."

Both men laughed. "Now let's grab our wives and go back to the palace and celebrate."

"Lead the way, Constantine."

An hour later they were all sitting around the table with their guests enjoying the food and drink that was being served to them. Anna had gone with Mary to their quarters to feed the baby. "You look very skeptical my friend." Colonel Longo said.

"What are you thinking, George."

"Sometimes I think I am dreaming all of this. I can't believe I am in Constantinopolis in the 15th century."

"You are my friend and thank the saints that god brought you here to save this city and resurrect the empire," the emperor said.

"Maybe it was a miracle that brought us here, your majesty. We could have ended up anywhere, instead fate brought us here."

"Historians and theologians will debate that for years to come. But thanks to you and your people with their knowledge and ideas this city and the empire has been reborn. Our economy is booming, we control a huge swath of land and our population is over a million people. This city has now grown to over 120,000."

"Our military is also one of the strongest in the world now, with the addition of thousands of former trained Ottoman troops that converted to Christianity."

"And they are excellent and well-disciplined soldiers, George" General Notaras added.

"Who knows what else we will find in the new mine tunnels that were recently discovered after they are dug out?"

"Let's hope we find more tech manuals and engineering equipment. Our economy is booming with the advent of new technologies now used for peaceful purposes. Our first railroad is being built thanks to Burns and Jenkins with their new locomotive design that copied one of your first steam train engines called the rocket. The track will reach Andrianoupolis in a few weeks. The train is already hauling cargo and passengers."

"We will build more railroads your majesty. We will connect the empire with railroads that will drastically improve the economy and enable our troops to deploy much faster. Now that our metallurgical experts have found a way to make copper wire cheaply, we will soon start building a telegraph network to communicate with all our cities and outposts throughout the empire."

"The railroads and faster communication will in fact bring prosperity to our people, George. Also for the first time in centuries, we have peace and no enemies. Out former enemies want to become allies. Who would ever have believed that would happen?"

"This is an opportunity we should not squander, your majesty."

"Especially after the Panagia saved their flagship and two merchant ships that were being attacked by three Mameluke (Egyptian) pirate warships south of Rhodes last month," Admiral

Laskaris said. "The Ottoman admiral hugged and kissed Lieutenant Speliotis, the Panagia's captain for saving their ass."

"That is a first."

"It is your majesty. The Mamelukes have also been harassing our trade in the southern Aegean. Maybe we should propose a joint expedition to eradicate the Mameluke pirate bases in Syria. It will be a good shake-down cruise for the Empress Mary. We want to get all the bugs out of her before we send her across the Atlantic."

"That is a great idea admiral. I will propose it to the Ottoman Ambassador later this afternoon. Hopefully we can mount a joint military expedition against a common enemy."

"We will be ready, your majesty."

"This will help the crew train for their long voyage."

"The frigate and crew will be ready to sail for the area you call Texas and Mexico by the end of the year. By early next year we will have another frigate commissioned."

"That will coincide with the end of the storm season that affects the region. General Mavrakis and my wife mentioned that Atlantic storms can be so severe with 150 mile an hour winds that can push the sea miles inland and sink most sailing ships."

"A lot will ride with that mission," said George. "We must be prepared for it and also have our house in order here with the Ottomans."

"This is why I will meet with their trade delegation. They would like to propose a joint project to build a railroad from Sinope to their capital."

"Seems, they too see the value in a railroad."

"I am sure Jeanie pointed out the commercial and military values of a rail road to her husband," George said.

"I will give them a positive response as long as they are willing to finance the project. We help them build it and sell them the technology. Prosperity will also be good for them. They have kept their word so far and pulled their forces back 100 miles along the Aegean shore as agreed in the treaty."

"There will be many engineering and technological challenges that will need to be overcome but together we will manage them. Will also propose that they send scholars to our new University of Constantinopolis and we send to theirs."

"That is a good idea, your majesty," George said.

"Ah, here come our ladies," said the emperor.

The two women walked in and chased away the orchestra playing Byzantine chamber music. Both the empress and Anna were in a festive mood to party. Mary had brought her portable DVD/CD player and put on an old KC and the sunshine band CD.

"Now who's going to dance? Constantine come here."

"George, you can also come here and dance with your wife."

The two men looked at each other. I guess we got to go, but I don't know that strange dance. What is it?"

"It's called disco. Just follow your wife's moves." Within a few minutes, Constantine was dancing to the tune of "that's the way I like it.

"You are pretty good husband as a beginner."

"I have a good teacher."

Within fifteen minutes the rest of the guests were also dancing and having fun. Longo grabbed one of the buxom servers and took her to the dance floor, followed by Major Garibaldi and the rest of the Americans. The arrival of the Americans from the future had ensured that Byzantine society and the rest of the world had been changed forever.

CHAPTER 7

Western Anatolia
March 15, 1454

It had been a little over year since the end of hostilities and the initial peace treaty with the Ottomans. The Empire of Byzantium with Constantine XI and the Empress Mary at the helm was prospering and expanding as was the Ottoman Empire, their former enemy. During a joint military expedition in the fall against the Egyptian Mamelukes, the timely intervention of the Byzantine steam frigate Empress Mary proved pivotal in saving the Ottoman fleet and helping them capture the Syrian port of Latakia. During the battle an Ottoman galley had in turn saved the Byzantine flag ship from serious damage or destruction by interposing herself between the Empress Mary that had lost power due to a blown safety valve and a Mameluke fire ship. The sacrifice of the Ottoman commander to save a former enemy had finally removed any distrust and animosity the Byzantines had against their former adversary. Now a treaty of peace, cooperation and alliance would bind the two empires together. To cement this alliance Emperor Constantine accompanied by General George Mavrakis and his wife Anna would travel to the Ottoman capital by train to sign the new treaty.

George and his wife the former Doctor Anna Marone looked out the window as the arid Anatolian landscape passed by. The train pulled by a Rocket II locomotive, named The Istanbul

Express, after a famous train in a future timeline speed south towards the Ottoman capital of Konya, at a sedate 30 mph. They would be arriving at their destination within the hour. Everyone had boarded the train at the bustling Ottoman free trade port of Sinope, on the southern coast of the black sea after being transported there by the new Imperial Flagship and steam frigate the Roger Green. The warship had been named in honor of the father of the modern Byzantine navy who had been one of the airmen that had been transported into the past with George and the rest of the Americans.

George thought back at the incident that brought them back in time, it seemed like an eternity ago that the convoy he had been ordered to protect had been attacked in a Taliban ambush. Fleeing for their lives they had taken refuge in an old mine that had been used by the Soviets during their occupation of Afghanistan. A suicide bomber had detonated a car bomb at the entrance to the mine, trapping them under tons of rubble. Traveling deeper into the mine they discovered an underground tunnel housing a base left there by the Soviets. While exploring the complex they had found rooms filled supplies, weapons, large power storage batteries and a room filled with computers and other equipment. When the generator providing power to the complex was started the computers came to life and started a countdown. Once the countdown was completed it sent a huge power surge into the mountain that opened a wormhole that transported the entire complex back to 1452, arriving near the city of Constantinopolis shortly before the Ottoman attack that conquered what remained of the Byzantine Empire. After making contact with the Byzantines, they joined forces. Using the combined skills and knowledge of the fifteen American survivors, the highly educated and skillful Byzantines and the ex-Soviet weapons they found in the underground base, they were able to assist the Byzantines to build up their military to take on and defeat the Ottomans. The rest was history.

The railroad line between the Black sea port of Sinope and the Ottoman capital a true engineering marvel for the time had just been recently completed with the aid of Byzantine engineers and loans. Helping the Ottomans develop their trade and infrastructure would go a long way in ensuring peace and prosperity. With the advent of steam power with the knowledge brought by the Americans and their new found wealth, the Byzantines had embarked on an ambitious infrastructure building program to link the empire with railroads. This had already started paying dividends in more trade and business as transportation costs plummeted and goods were quickly and safely delivered.

The door car door opened and Constantine XI the emperor of the newly restored Byzantine Empire walked in. George stood up in respect for his commander and chief.

"No need to stand, please sit down, general. We will be in Konya shortly. Never in my wildest dreams did I expect to be signing a treaty of alliance with the Ottomans."

"This is a strange new world, your majesty. I'm sure we will see many weider things once deemed impossible in our lifetime."

"That is true my friend. Who ever thought of steamships, telegraph and railroads, in 1454?"

"If Jenkins can get the fuel mixture right on the Russian motors we will soon have an air force."

"It seems he is almost there. The small plane that Captain Fulton has built has been flown successfully. Granted, he has had a couple of close calls with the engine stalling in mid-flight."

"He should have the correct fuel mixture down pat in the next few days. We have so far found 30 engines in crates and we are still finding things in the caves. Seems the Russians had stored many items there. I believe they were planning to travel back in time and alter the future to make a Soviet communist empire that would rule the world."

"From what Mary told me they were evil and forbade the worship of god."

"That is correct, Constantine. When they first took power in 1917 during the first Great War, they killed all the nobility, the rich and priests."

"That was a terrible period but they did eventually collapse."

"Thank god for the world that they collapsed without a destructive nuclear war that may have ended life on earth."

"That is very true, Constantine."

"Anna you have been silent all this time are you okay?"

"I am fine Constantine. I just miss my daughter."

"She is in good hands with her godmother, she is fine."

"I know, but this is the first time I am away and I miss her."

"I am sure Mary would feel the same."

The train had entered the outskirts of Konya; George noticed that the track was lined on each side by heavy Sipahi cavalry serving as an honor guard. "Guess we should prepare to meet our young host."

"Yes, general. This should prove interesting."

The train stopped at the main station. An honor guard consisting of Janissaries dressed in ceremonial uniforms waited outside the train. Thousands of the town's residents were also there to witness this historical event. George could see that the soldiers were all armed with muskets sportung gleaming bayonets. That was indeed a surprise. When the emperor and his entourage stepped out of the train, they were met by the sultan and his wife Janie the new sultana. Several commands were issued by the officer commanding the honor guard. The honor guard quickly came to attention and presented arms. George was impressed even more so when he noticed that the weapons were flintlocks.

"Welcome to my capital, Constantine. I will always be indebted to you for what you did for me and my people, after everything that I had done to you and your city. I would have never shown you mercy. You are a better man then I. Let us shake for a new beginning," the sultan held out his hand.

The Byzantine Emperor stared at the sultan and hesitated for a moment but took the young man's hand and shook it warmly. "If that was an apology Mehmet, I accept it. Yes, let's shake on a new alliance between our two great powers."

The Sultan then went over and shook George's hand and hugged Anna and thanked her again for saving his life and giving him another opportunity to be a ruler. "I can never thank you enough, doctor, for saving my life and giving me another chance. I will always be in your debt and that of your husband's."

"I now know I did the right thing, Mehmet. You better though take good care of my girlfriend" She hugged the young man and kissed his cheek, causing him to blush. Then she went over and hugged her friend, Janie.

"Welcome Anna, I missed you."

"I missed you to."

"I can't wait for you to see my son." She pulled out a cell phone and showed her a picture of an infant."

"What a cute little boy."

"His name is Bayazid, Giorgios. I also named him in honor of your husband who saved his father's life."

"Please everyone let's go to my palace for some food and refreshments."

They boarded a closed ornate carriage and were transported to a very large building in which parts of it were covered with scaffolding, where construction workers still labored. Constantine's Imperial body guards were given horses to accompany the carriage and rode side by side with the sultan's Sipahi guard. When the carriage came to a halt, its occupants got out and were escorted by the sultan's private guard to the inner chambers. George was amazed at the opulence of the inside of the palace. Beautiful tapestries adorned the marble walls as did silk rugs the floors. Various ancient Greek works of art were displayed in every room; finally they entered a large room adorned with a beautiful marble table that was full of food and drink.

"Please my friends have a seat. My grand vizier will soon join us."

As if on cue Zaganos Pasha, the Sultan's grand vizier entered the room. He walked up to the emperor and bowed deeply. "Welcome to our capital. I hope your trip here will usher in a new era in our evolving relationship.'

"I pray to god that it will. Our two peoples' have much to offer and learn from each other."

"Indeed they do. The empire also wishes to thank its Byzantine brothers, for making our victory possible in Syria."

"Yes, Constantine, the timely arrival of your steam frigate pulled our nuts out of the fire, as my wife would say. You saved my fleet and ensured our victory at Latakia."

"That's what friends and allies do, Mehmet."

"Yes, that is what allies are supposed to do. I am learning this. Now please enjoy the food and drink."

After the rich banquet, Anna went with Janie to the royal quarters to see her baby while the men retired with their staff to a conference room to discuss the new treaty of alliance. The sultan was the first to speak since he was hosting the conference.

"Gentlemen, after several weeks of discussions between our two staffs, we are ready to sign a treaty of alliance and cooperation between our two empires. I must admit that there may still be some mistrust between us. I do sincerely hope after the successful Syrian military campaign most of the mistrust has gone away. We desire to usher a new era of cooperation amongst our two empires in trade, science and military advancement. We are beholden to you in many ways. You could have destroyed us but you did not. You chose to save my life and help my people. We owe you a great debt. With the construction of the new railroad, we have been able to double our trade. We thank you for assisting us in building this great technological project. The world has in the last couple of years been drastically changed with the arrival of General Mavrakis and his people. Military weaponry has been advanced hundreds of years in the space of only a couple. Presently Byzantium may hold the lead in military superiority but it's only a matter of time before other nations catch up. My spies tell me the Venetians are mounting guns on their ships and equipping their infantry with fire arms. You will be in direct competition with the Venetians in Greece and the Aegean. It's only a matter of time before your interests clash. We will soon begin a campaign of evicting the Mamelukes from the holy land. We are willing to share the holy city of Jerusalem with you. It should be a city where all religions can worship freely and in peace. We are also looking to explore and spread our empire. I know you will find us trustworthy and loyal allies." The sultan bowed towards the emperor and sat down.

Constantine stood up and looked at his audience for a moment. A little more than a year ago, these same people were trying to kill him now they wanted to be friends and allies. What a strange world he thought. "My friends this is a strange new world indeed. A little more than a year ago, you were trying to kill us, now we are here as friends and allies, thanks to General Mavrakis and his people from the future. In fact two of them became our lovely wives. Thanks to them we are both alive and both our nations are in a better position to confront this new world. One thing my religion teaches us is to show mercy and forgive. I have forgiven you for all that has happened between us. Now I look forward in friendship and cooperation between our two great states. As a token of our friendship we are suspending the last installment of war reparations. It will be better used in building your infrastructure. What you said is true. There are many enemies out there that will look to exploit any weakness. I will accept a joint administration of Jerusalem and the rest of the land that will be known in the future as Israel. We will contribute troops to help you liberate the land. Together we have the ability to change the world for the better. In May we are sending an expedition to the Americas. I am offering you to send a mission along." That brought a murmur from the Ottoman delegation. The expedition will go to Mexico. A warlike people called the Aztecs that make humans sacrifices to their sun god, live there. They have untold riches in gold and jewels."

"Human, sacrifices! In the name of Allah, these infidels must be destroyed," said the grand Mufti of Konya.

"Yes, your Excellency, they are very evil and in the name of god must be eradicated or converted to one of the religions of the book."

"Yes, they are an abomination and must be dealt with.

"General Mavrakis, will you please continue."

George stood up and took the floor. "The two great continents of North and South America as they will be called in my timeline hold untold riches and lie out there, ripe for the picking. It will not be too long before the other European nations mount expeditions there. There are many resources there that we can use. One of these key resources is oil. It will be the life blood of future economies. Wars will be fought for this key resource in my time. There is oil much closer we will need to secure in the immediate future. Unfortunately the Arabs presently own it and are supported by the Mamelukes. Much of it lies in the Middle East in Saudi Arabia or where Mecca and Medina lie and there are huge deposits in Mesopotamia and Persia." He showed them on an IPAD that he had with him maps of the area.

"The entire Saudi peninsula is floating in oil. In my timeline the Ottomans eventually captured it in the early 16th century. There is oil closer in south east Romania, in an area called Ploesti; we intend to capture it in the next few years. Presently we are receiving small shipments of oil from an area called Baku in the Black sea region by trading with the Shirvan khanate who rule the area. We have made them an offer to build a trading post and let us drill for oil. We believe they will accept it.

"What does oil do? How do you make it into fuel?" The grand vizier asked.

The petroleum must be refined, which is boiling it to a high temperature and made into fuel to power machines and weapons of war."

"That is true, Mehmet. Janie has taught you much," George said with a smile.

"Without it wars will be lost in the future," the sultan added.

"We will secure Saudi Arabia as soon as possible but we need to secure Egypt first. If you assist us we will capture Egypt much faster."

"Thank you, General Mavrakis, the emperor said.

"I will consider it, Mehmet. Your proposal to secure Egypt does have merit. As for oil refining we still need to make a few breakthroughs in chemistry and engineering to be able to refine the oil to fuel. We have already begun experiments. I propose we establish a chemical engineering department in both our new universities and that we send our best and brightest there to research oil refining. Also there is much oil to be found in an area that will be called Texas. It's the south west gulf region of America." The emperor pointed Mexico and Texas out on the IPAD and showed them maps of the world. "Gentlemen you can see from these maps that the new world is long voyage, almost 11000 kilometers. In the summer and fall months the coastal regions are hit by huge storms with winds in excess of 200 kilometers an hour. The sea can be pushed inland for kilometers."

"They are called hurricanes. My wife said one hit a large city called New Orleans with a wind speed of over 300 kilometers an hour and caused a ten meter storm surge that drowned over 1000 people." This brought gasps from almost everyone there.

"Yes your eminence it was called Hurricane Katrina. In the early 20th century a Hurricane hit a small city in Texas and drowned almost 10,000 people. They can be very deadly so we must be careful with the weather. The best place for a ship in a hurricane is to ride it out at sea. We will be taking two frigates, so we will have engine power in case we are caught in a storm. This increases our survival odds much more than being at the mercy of the wind."

"Thank you General Mavrakis. The general knows the region and will command the expedition. I propose that an Ottoman be the deputy commander of this expedition to solidify our alliance. We eventually can secure the area and its resources for our future. Join us; there is a continent to take. We need to get there first. Thank you."

With that, the emperor sat down and the room erupted in applause. "Thank you, Emperor Constantine, you are a true friend. The Ottomans will remember this day for generations to come. Everything you said is true Constantine and has great merit. First we will agree to joint rule in the lands of Palestine. We will join you on your expedition to the Americas. It's an honor that you asked us to come along and more so offering the deputy command to an Ottoman officer. I will give you Ismail Bay and a detachment of my elite Janissary palace guard."

"That will be excellent." George said.

"We understand Constantine, that the real road to power is science and a strong economy. My people must make rapid scientific advancements in chemistry and medicine. We will create a new chemical engineering department in our new university and you are more than welcome to send scholars. Sharing your medical advances has already saved hundreds of lives at our hospitals and infant mortality has dropped by 70%. We too want to be part of the cutting edge of science and technology. We will join you and send our best and brightest to Constantinopolis to make this happen.

After the speeches both Emperor Constantine and the sultan signed the treaty of friend ship and alliance. It was now up to the various staff officers and diplomats on both sides to implement it. After the signing, everyone went to the banquet hall for food and entertainment. The cuisine was excellent consisting of wild game and roast lamb, various rice pilafs topped with numerous sweet honey pastries like baklava. George filled two plates and walked over to where Anna was sitting.

"Mmmm, that food looks delicious." Anna put a forkful in her mouth. "It is delicious."

"Well the Turkish cuisine is one of the best in the world. Just wait till they discover tomatoes."

"I can see why. It will be soon. Ottoman traders have already purchased tomato seedlings and have begun to grow them locally."

"Well my dear it's done we are now allies with the Ottomans. Constantine has even invited them to the America expedition."

"Once he was sold on the idea, he has taken this alliance to heart. I'm sure Mary has been an influence."

"As has Janie on her husband."

"It's better to be friends and share the wealth then to be at constant war and have nothing."

"That is a good point, Anna."

"I hope you are enjoying the food?"

Both Anna and George looked up and saw the grand vizier. "I apologize if I am disturbing you."

"Why of course not, the Ottoman Grand Vizier is always welcome at our table. Please have a seat."

"Thank you, Madam."

"Please call me, Anna."

"I want to thank you both for supporting this treaty. Without you it never would have happened."

"It's better to be friends then enemies."

"That is a fact and my people are finding this out. We are a race of warriors. We used to ride across the steeps raiding and conquering. Now war must only be used as a last resort. My people are learning this."

"That is a good thing, Zaganos Pasha."

"Yes it is. Thanks to you, my people will now become explorers, engineers and scientists. They will even travel to the Americas."

"It is a huge continent and there is room for everyone."

"My sultan is giving you Ismail Bey. He is a good man and very loyal. You can trust him with your life. Without him the Sultan would now be dead and the Ottomans in a civil war. Ismail stood by him and gave him support of his army, till Mehmet was able to consolidate his rule. Even though he has divorced his sister, the sultan has kept him as his second vizier to reward him for his loyalty."

"Thank you for telling me this. The trip there will be long dangerous and not all the natives will be friendly. I will need good soldiers."

"You will get 200 of our best Janissary palace guard; they will serve you loyally till death."

"Let's hope we don't get to that point. I want all of us to come back in one piece."

"Both our priests and imams will pray for this, but this mission will be fraught with risks. I wish I was a younger man and free from responsibilities. I would want to come along."

"I would love to have you with us. Your wisdom and opinions would be most valued."

"Thank you my friend but I must remain here with the young sultan and give him advice. He is still not totally secure on his throne. There are still rogue elements that hold our recent defeat, against him and are against this alliance."

"Not everyone in Byzantium is thrilled either, but we have to give peace a chance in this new world. We have too many enemies to be fighting amongst ourselves."

"Yes you make a good point but there are always those that will disagree."

"Yes as long as they don't choose violence to make their point."

"We will need your help to secure the holy land from the Mamelukes. My sultan has offered a joint administration."

"Yes that is a great proposal and I will speak to the emperor about. Hopefully we can move quickly before the Mamelukes recover. Jerusalem should be a city where all faiths are welcome and free to worship. We can make millions in tourism from all the visitors that will come. Imagine it taverns and hostels for all the faithful to visit and worship in peace.

"Yes that would be something. Well enjoy your dinner. I have taken enough of your time."

"You are welcome anytime at our table."

"Thank you, doctor."

Two hours later both George and Anna were in the sultan's quarters visiting Janie and her new baby. "Well we know whom he gets his good looks from."

"It's obviously his mother," said the sultan who was proudly holding his son.

"He is also healthy as an ox." Anna said having examined the child earlier and given him a small pox vaccination."

"Our medicine has improved much with the help of your physicians and the new medical school and drug lab you helped us set up."

"Medicine will even improve much more, Mehmet, as we develop more medicines and better doctors."

"That is not the only thing that has improved Mehmet. You have come a long way in a little over a year. You have made great advances in infrastructure, education, science and trade."

"I have to thank my wife who has taught me much of the future and better ways of ruling a nation. Greatness is not only being known as conqueror. I want to go down in history as an enlightened ruler and leave a legacy and a great nation for my son to rule."

"You have indeed become a wise man and ruler my friend."

"Thank you, General Mavrakis."

"Please call me, George."

"Thank you George. I wish I was going with you to the new world. Unfortunately, I can't leave my wife alone to rule here. There is too much intrigue going on."

"Yes, I know I have heard."

The sultan smiled. "You have been speaking to my grand vizier. He is a very wise man."

"Yes he is and a good man. The same intrigue but to a lesser degree is also happening in Constantinoplis. There are those that believe we should have totally crushed you so the Ottomans could never become a threat again. Constantine will not have anything to do with that. He is totally committed to friendship and alliance."

"I thank all of you for that. Together we can create a great economic block in this part of the world and expand to the new world."

"We need to become manufacturing centers and sell to the world. But we will not sell weapons. Though the genie is out of the bottle, we will try to keep our military secrets out of the hands of our enemies for as long as possible."

"All the major powers will soon be building advanced weapons but maybe we can slow down the arms race. We too are using steam power to increase our production in the new factories we are building. Our first steam war ship will be launched very shortly and we will be building more for trade. Hopefully within a year we will build a steam frigate to be able to join you in the Americas."

A knock on the door momentarily interrupted their conversation. "My padishah, the Byzantine Emperor has arrived."

"Show him in."

A moment later Emperor Constantine was escorted into the royal quarters, holding an ornate wooden box. "What is that my friend."

"A small gift for the future sultan," he replied as he opened the box and pulled out a jewel encrusted pendent showing the Byzantine eagles flying toward a moon and crescent.

"That's so beautiful," said Julie

"Maybe one day man will travel earlier to the moon."

"That may happen a lot sooner. Byzantium will soon have an air force."

"What? You will have aircraft?"

"We had originally found twelve small car motors. Subsequently we found a new shaft that had been buried from a cave in. We found many more things there, to include thirty five more engines, heavy weapons and equipment, ammunition, generators a technology library and a large underground deposit of gasoline. The Soviets as they were called were definitely planning something."

"Ir seems so, Constantine. That Soviet underground base is massively changing history."

Captain Fulton has designed an aircraft and mounted an engine."

"Does it fly?"

"Yes it does Mehmet. We've even mounted light bombs and a machine gun on it."

"In the name of the prophet, man flying! That is unbelievable."

"With an air force we are now the most powerful nation in the world. Once we translate the Russian technical and scientific manuals, we will be able to rapidly improve or industry and technology."

Constantine saw both the look of fear and surprise on the sultan's face. Of course we will train two Ottoman pilots and give you two aircraft for now."

"You will give us an airplane?"

"Yes Mehmet, we are now allies."

The sultan was flabbergasted and dropped to his knees. "Thank you my friend. I will be forever indebted to you. This will go a long way in stabilizing my rule and cementing our alliance with my military."

"We have also begun building an airship using water proof gas bags and Hydrogen gas to use for trade and transportation."

"I remember seeing those on Julies IPAD. They were used during your first great war. Mankind is really moving forward."

"The world will soon become much smaller with air travel and steam ships. We have sent out trading missions to England and several to Asia around the horn of Africa."

"We too will soon be sending out a trade missions to various parts of the world."

"We have also found twenty wireless radios with batteries wind and hand generators. We have brought one for you with two NCOs to train your men. With it we can keep in constant contact and we may be even able to communicate with our expedition in the new world."

"I must thank you again Constantine for your generosity."

"We need to have open communications between us at all times and we need to have communications with our people in the new world."

"Will these radios reach that far?"

"They will need to have tall antennas. We will show you how to set them up and use them. They are short wave radios, if the conditions are right the signals will bounce off the earth's atmosphere, George answered."

"So they will not always reach here?"

"No, not always."

There was a knock on the door and a steward entered with fresh pastries and refreshments. "Please enjoy some refreshments and pastries before you retire for the night. We have a long day ahead tomorrow."

"Thank you, my padishah. I think I will," Anna said bringing a laugh to everyone there.

Chapter 8

Constantinopolis
18 April 1454

George looked towards the dark area of land that was fading in the distance. He was in the control gondola of the Icarus, Byzantium's new airship cruising westwards over the Aegean sea at an airspeed of 100 kilometers an hour and at an altitude of 1000 meters. Captain Fulton was at the helm of his latest 50 meter long flying invention. They were coming up fast on the Byzantine and Ottoman naval flotilla that had left the city of Smyrna, the night before for Palestine. Leading that fleet were the steam gunboats Niki and Sultana Julie.

"I still can't believe we are flying my friend. Never in my life could I have even imagined the concept of man flying," said Giustiaianini Longo, the former Genovese commander who had fought bravely with his men during the siege and helped save Constantinopolis.

"Well colonel we are in fact flying."

"There they are, sir. I told you we would quickly find them. Even at this low altitude we can see for many miles. "

"That you did captain."

"Sir, I've spotted several other sails just to the north," said one of the five crew members that were serving as a look out.

George took his binoculars and looked towards the northern horizon and spotted several sails. "Fulton, turn the ship towards the north and head for those sails."

"Yes, sir."

The 160 foot airship with a large Byzantine flag painted on each side turned slowly towards the north. Ten minutes later the ships, five large galleasses with several smaller galleys came into view. "I see their flag; it's our "friends" the Venetians."

"They're shadowing our invasion fleet, colonel. Interesting they are all armed with cannon. Not as good as ours but still canon."

"What did you expect sir? The genie is out of the bottle. Thank god we now have an air force."

"Fulton, take us down to 500 meters and fly over the flagship. It's that one in the middle with the admiral's pennant."

Fulton put the Icarus in a shallow dive and flew towards the flagship. He peered through his glasses as the ship grew larger. The crew was in a panic having never seen a flying machine before." Several puffs of smoke were seen coming from the deck of the flagship.

"They are shooting at us, sir."

"They must be scared out of their minds"

"They'll be even more terrified now having seen the Byzantine markings on the ship."

"They are shadowing our invasion fleet. Take us over our flagship we need to let the Admiral know."

"Aye, aye, sir."

"Fulton. Give me a pencil, paper and a waterproof bag. I need to write a message to the admiral. Would have been nice had we had a radio installed."

"That will be done next week, sir.

"Venice will not be very happy once we take the holy land."

"I don't see why not we are going to treat everyone equal."

"They figure they should be the rightful owners and protectors of the holy lands."

"Well that's not going to happen and they are in no position to challenge us. Especially after seeing this this airship they will think twice before they try anything. I'm sure their admiral will be dispatching a ship to tell Venice of the airship's existence."

Fifteen minutes later the Itcarus hovered over the Niki and dropped a weighted bag on the deck of the flagship. "The Admiral's got the message the he is being followed. Do we have enough fuel to make it back to the capital?"

"Yes sir we'll make it"

"Take us home, captain."

Five hours later the Icarus was being pulled into its hanger at the newly built Constantinopolis air base. A carriage was waiting for George and Colonel Longo to transport them to headquarters. George glanced outside and saw several F1 Pegasus fighters parked next to the hanger they just left, one of them having Ottoman markings was revving its engine. It was piloted by Lieutenant Ozal, the Ottoman Empires first pilot. When they arrived at headquarters, they were met by the commander and chief Emperor Constantine and General Notaras chairman of the joint chiefs.

"Greetings, gentlemen. How was your flight?"

"It was fantastic your majesty! I never dreamed I would one day be flying like the birds."

"The world is changing, colonel. We must be ready to quickly adopt."

"We spotted the Venetian fleet tailing our invasion fleet."

"Yes, Admiral Laskaris reported the contact. He will keep an eye on them. There is not much we can do if they want to follow our ships."

"No, there isn't your majesty; we just keep an eye on them. They won't do anything, not after they saw the Icarus. We have the ability to destroy their navy from the air."

"That is true, George. I will hate to not have you and Colonel Longo, here for almost a year."

"We need to get across the Atlantic and lay claim to the new world before someone else gets there first.

"I know my friend and I wish you luck over there. I wish I could go with you."

"We need you here to watch over the empire and our alliance and to take care of my family."

"Don't worry about that. Your family will be safe as will the empire. Most of your men will stay here and we will continue with our technological, military and economic advances."

"We need those Russian books translated. There is a lot of information there we can use in chemistry, metallurgy and Petroleum refining. The Soviets were planning something big. The volumes of information there contain enough info to create a modern world."

"We have brought Russ speakers but the books are written in modern Russian and they don't understand many of the terms so this will take a long time. Oh, I almost forgot. Your Ottoman contingent will be arriving tomorrow."

"That's good to know I will meet them on the docks. We have a few weeks to train them and bring them up to speed before we sail. We will issue them Nagants and AK47s. The Nagant rounds are the easiest to reload and we have found lots of bullets in the underground base."

"Train them well George, you will be heavily outnumbered and thousands of miles from supplies and reinforcements. Your men well need to be able to handle any situation that arises in the new world."

"I to wish I was a younger man to sail with you to a new world."

"You too are needed here, General Notaras. We need to keep modernizing the army. I don't trust the Venice."

"They would not dare do anything. Not with the Ottomans as our allies."

"They too can get allies," Colonel Longo added. "Do not drop your guard one minute gentlemen when we are gone. Venice wants control of the Mediterranean she can't have it. They will now look elsewhere."

"We have heard rumors they too want to mount an expedition to the new world. They have been hiring ship builders and will pay lots of gold to build a ship to cross the Atlantic."

"We will get there first. Now gentlemen go get something to eat and get some rest. Tomorrow will be a long day after our allies arrive."

Constantinopolis, Naval Station
19 April 1454

The Byzantine gun boat Elli pulled into the naval station with the Ottoman contingent it had picked up at the Sinope rail road siding. First off the boat was its commanding officer and the deputy commander of the expedition, Brigadier General Ismail Bey who was then followed by the rest of the Ottoman troops. George was impressed with the quality of the troops who were smartly dressed in olive drab combat gear with steel pots on the heads and armed with flintlock muskets. The allied troops were quickly formed up in five rows by their officers and NCO's facing the Imperial honor guard. The Ottoman's had also converted to the American rank system by Julie's urging, in the effort to develop a professional military. Ismail Bey walked up to George and saluted then hugged him. "Thank you for the honor guard, my friend. I bring you greetings from my sultan. He wishes you and your family well. I am also honored to be here."

"I am also honored to have you as my second in command, Ismail. You and your men must be tired. My men will escort your officers and men to their barracks. I will show you to your quarters in the palace. There will be a banquet in your honor tonight. All your officers are also welcome."

"Of course, we will all be there, general. I love good food and drink."

"There will be plenty food there."

"Now would you like to inspect your troops, general?"

"My troops? Um, yes, it would be an honor."

Ismail Bay turned around and gave the troops the order to prepare for inspection. Ryan was impressed, Julie had taught them well. He heard that she was commanding their military academy. After finishing the inspection George marched to the head of the formation and requested that the troops be put at parade rest so he could speak to them. General Ismail bay gave the command for parade rest.

"Welcome to Constantinoplis. You have been chosen, because you are some of the best soldiers the Ottoman Empire has to offer. I am proud to be your commander for this dangerous and historic mission to the new world. We will be gone for almost a year and be thousands of miles away from our home base. The mission will be fraught with danger and many unknowns. We must learn to trust and depend on one another. You have four weeks to train and learn some of the skills that will help you survive. You will all be issued modern fire arms and ammunition and trained in their use. This will give you a better chance of survival if it comes to a fight. My self and General Ismail Bay will try to get everyone back in one piece, but no one knows what fate will have in store for all of us. Now my officers will escort you to your barracks where you can freshen up and enjoy the food and drink and meet your Byzantine brothers in arms whom you will be training with and will be accompanying you on this dangerous mission. I welcome you to the expedition and may the lord of the heavens and the prophet protect us all. Now enjoy yourselves, the training starts tomorrow. General Ismail Bay the troops are yours."

"Thank you general, Mavrakis." Ismail Bay turned command over to his officers who began marching the troops to their new quarters.

"Now please General Ismail Bay, accompany me to the palace."

"Please general, call me Ismail."

"You can also call me, George. Now lets go get cleaned up and have something to eat."

"Lead the way."

Both men got in one of the ex-Soviet GAZ 69 jeeps that had been found in the underground base and were driven to the palace where Ismail bay was shown to his quarters.

A few hours later George and Anna showed up to the banquet which was being held in honor of Ismail Bay. The tables were packed with roast, lamb, chicken, burgers and all sorts of pastries. They were both escorted to the official table were the Imperial couple were sitting, in the company of Colonel Longo and Ismail bay with several of his officers. The Turkish contingent got up and was introduced to George. He was especially impressed with Lieutenant Colonel Ali Pasha whom he had met earlier. Rumor had it that during the siege of Constantinopolis, he had been in command of a Janissary detachment and had been one of the first units to plant their flag on the City walls. There was no doubt of this man's bravery.

The jovial Ismail Bay hugged Anna and gave her a kiss on the cheek. This is from the sultana; she wishes she could be here too."

"Thank you, Ismail. I wish my friend was here too." Anna then took a seat next to her friend the empress Mary and a former USAF non-commissioned officer. George took a seat next to Longo and Lt. Colonel Ali Pasha. Across him sat both the emperor and General Ismail Bay.

"General Mavrakis you were right, the food is indeed excellent especially the hamburgers! The sultana has also introduced hamburgers into the Turkish cuisine."

"Wait till you start using tomatoes and tomato sauce. Your cuisine will become one of the best in the world," George added.

"I hear there are many more treats that await us in the new world such as chocolate and tobacco," Colonel Ali said.

"That is true and thousands of savage natives will be waiting to capture us and sacrifice us to their gods."

"I do not fear them. My men and I will send the heathen unbelievers to hell."

"Your bravery is legendary, colonel. I have heard of your combat exploits and I am honored to have you with us, but we will have to be smart. We can't afford to fight everyone. We must fight intelligently because we will have limited supplies and man power. When we lose a man we can't replace him but the savages can replace one of theirs' with thousands."

"Thank you, sir. Obviously, you know my men were the first to breach your walls and penetrate deep into the city, had it not been for your intervention with your infernal fighting machine, we would have defeated you and you would have been our slaves."

George and the others who had heard what the colonel had said stopped talking and starred at him. "But by the will of Allah that was not what he had in store for us. We were defeated by your superior military technology and the bravery of your soldiers. You treated us honorably even saving the life of our sultan and gave the Ottomans another chance to be a great power once again. This is a much better future than the one that we would have had in your timeline. Look at us now, we are allies and are accompanying you to the new world, to equally enjoy its riches. The old Ottoman Empire would have been locked in perpetual wars and finally decay and collapse having contributed almost nothing to the world. We now have been given another chance. Thank you for that chance my friends."

The emperor stood up and began to clap and was soon joined by the rest of the room. He raised his goblet, "long live sultan Mehmet."

Everyone stood up and toasted the sultan. General Ismail Bay raised his wine goblet and toasted the emperor. George was positive that any animosity between the two sides was no longer there.

Sea of Marmara
May 4, 1454

The 1500-ton steam frigate Empress Mary was a mile off the coast bobbing up and down in the early morning swells. The sun would soon be coming up as the eight man commando team made up of four Byzantines and four Ottomans were transported to shore in one of the Russian Zodiacs they had found in the in the underground base. The inflatable surged ahead at a steady 25 miles per hour powered by a Johnson 50hp outboard motor. Five minutes later the team had hit the beach Colonel Longo was leading the team with Colonel Ali Pasha serving as an ordinary team member. Their object was to simulate blowing up a bridge, guarded by a platoon of Imperial Guards. There second target was capturing the entrance to the Russian underground base.

"Let's get going men I want to hit the bridge at sunrise. That's when sentries are the most vulnerable. The bridge is about five kilometers distant; we should be there in about an hour."

"Isn't this the bridge that was blown up during the war?"

"Yes, it is Colonel. Let's see if we can do it again."

The sun was just beginning to break when they reached the bridge. The team quickly went into action. Longo sent two men at each end to neutralize the sentries which they quickly did. Within ten minutes the bridge was wired with a simulated demolition charge. Just as the team finished a guard patrol showed up. While they noticed the missing sentries, they also found the note Longo left next to the simulated explosives package.

"Good job men. We just rubbed the noses of the Imperial Guards into the dirt. Let's head for our next target."

"Maybe we'll get there for a late breakfast, colonel."

"We'll give it our best shot, Colonel."

Two and a half hours later the team had reached the vicinity of the mine entrance. The team had maneuvered to the top of the hill right above the mine's entrance. After the war the entrance to the mine had been fortified with a guard post and a machine gun bunker. The only way that Longo had a chance was to repel from the top of the hill onto the bunker. Everyone carried an AK47 with a magazine of blank ammo that they had found in the underground base. Only Longo carried a pistol with live ammo.

"This is it men. Let's do it on three. One, two, three!" Six men repelled off the side of the hill. Longo landed on top of the bunker and lobed a training grenade into the opening. Colonel Ali landed on his feet firing the AK47 in short bursts which if the bullets were real would have taken out the sentries. In less than ten seconds the entrance was taken.

"We did it! Now let's go inside. You will see lots of strange things inside the main base."

"Don't worry colonel, nothing surprises us anymore after seeing flying machines," Colonel Ali said.

Longo and the rest of the commandos climbed aboard a jeep and drove into the mine. Within ten minutes they had reached the interior of the main base and began to neutralize the armed sentries inside. Lieutenant Colonel Petros Tomas the base commander heard the commotion and rushed out of his office only to be taken prisoner by Longo.

"I believe the base is ours."

"I believe it is, sir. You took the base fair and square."

"Colonel Ali and I will write an after action report and recommend security improvements."

"That will be greatly appreciated, gentlemen."

"Have you met Colonel Ali?"

"Yes, we met at headquarters last week when I was on a supply run to the city."

"One action you could take immediately colonel is to place sentries on the top of the hill. That is your Achilles heel as you Greeks would say."

"Noted, Colonel Ali. Now would you like something to eat and have a tour of the base?"

"I am sure the men are starving. We would appreciate that very much Colonel Tomas. So far of what I have seen in here is utterly fantastic."

After a breakfast of eggs and pancakes with honey, Colonel Ali and his men were given a tour of the underground installation by Colonel Tomas and recently promoted Major Jenkins who was at the base designing metal dyes to make 5.56mm and 7.62mm ammo. "This place is amazing! Lights, generators, advanced weaponry and repair facilities."

"Yes colonel, it is truly amazing. We are constantly finding new hiding places containing equipment. We found several more engines, large rolls of wire, two generators, several more radios and wind and hand generators and batteries for them. We also found several oil drills, ammunition reloading kits, light mortars, machine guns and ammo and another diesel and gasoline storage area. We even found a couple of canons, 76 mm divisional guns M1942 (ZiS-3). They were in pieces in wooden boxes. We also found about 300 rounds. It seems the Soviets that built this place were storing enough equipment here to keep a small army running for years."

"We'll never know what they were planning. The more equipment we find the faster we can all modernize."

"We will keep searching the tunnels, gentlemen. We have just found another tunnel that is blocked by a cave in. Miners will be brought in here to help dig it out. Who knows what we will find in there?"

"Byzantium can destroy all their enemies with the contents of this base."

"The equipment is limited, colonel. Once it's broken or the ammo is used then it's useless. We must learn to produce it. This is why we are pushing technology and education."

"As is the Ottoman state, Major Jenkins. We will not be the same Ottoman empire that existed in your previous timeline"

"Even our enemies are doing the same, sir. Knowledge is power."

"That is why we must keep it as much of it within our two states."

"We can't keep it secret forever, sir. It will leak out to our enemies. That is why we must always be in the cutting edge of technology.

"I would like to return to the city before sundown."

"I will have the Humvee drive you to the city."

"Thank you, Colonel Tomas that would be very much appreciated. We all thank you for your hospitality."

Constantinopolis, Naval Station
May 15, 1494

The day had finally arrived for the expedition's departure for the new world. Both frigates the Empress Mary and the newer frigate the Limnos, armed with 24 of the latest 32 pounder naval guns had just finished a two week overhaul that included an engine upgrade for the Empress Mary. The mixed contingent of 400 Byzantine and Ottoman troops stood in the parade ground. Next to them was a ten man cavalry scout contingent that was also coming along. Five of the horses were male and the other five females. They would be released in in the new world and left to procreate. Within a generation there would be hundreds if not thousands of horses running wild. They had been joined by Lieutenant Leroy Davis who would be acting as George's adjutant. Both George and Brigadier General Ismail Bay stood in front of the contingent and faced the VIP platform awaiting the speeches from the dignitaries. Late yesterday afternoon, the airship Icarus had arrived from the Ottoman capital carrying the sultan and his entourage. The young man had been ecstatic during the entire flight, especially when Captain Fulton had given him the controls. The sultan decided then and there that he would one day learn to fly. The emperor walked up to the podium. A cone had been erected by the podium to help amplify the speaker's voice.

"My friends before I continue, I would like to announce that our forces have captured Jerusalem, the holy city for the three great religions of the world." A cheer erupted from everyone there. "

"Now back to our original mission. We are all here today to wish our soldiers good luck on this great journey of exploration to the new world across the great Atlantic Ocean. You will face great dangers and meet new enemies but you have the strength, training and equipment that will help you prevail. You will discover many new things there that will help both our great empires grow and become richer and more powerful. The lands you claim will eventually be colonized by our people. We will spread across two continents. History is being re written as we speak. None of us know the future. But I do know one thing. We will make a new future." The emperor motioned for the young sultan to join him. Just as he walked over to the podium there was the sound of approaching aircraft from the west everyone looked up to see an overflight of ten Pegasus F1 monoplane fighters, two of them with Ottoman markings.

"I am proud to finally be in Constantinopolis, not as a

conqueror but friend and ally. When I looked up in the sky to see two aircraft bearing Ottoman markings, I felt real pride to be the only other nation on earth to have machines that fly. These machines were given to us by a true friend. What the emperor said is true. You will all face great dangers but the rewards you will reap for yourselves and your nations will be enormous. I wish I was going with you. This is only the beginning, one day we will send settlers there and build great cities. You are the vanguard that will make this happen. My soldiers take care of your comrades, you will be alone and far away, you will all need each other. Now go with Allah's blessing."

With the completion of the speeches both the Orthodox patriarch and the city's Imam gave a blessing before the men began boarding the two ships. George walked over to the VIP podium to where Anna was sitting with their daughter on her lap. George picked up the child and gave her a kiss then hugged his wife who was beginning to cry. "I'll be okay my love. I will be back to both of you."

"I know you will George. I can't help being worried. Please be careful George, we want you back in one peace."

"I will Anna."

"Here comes company." George looked up and saw the emperor and the sultan walking over.

"Don't worry general your family will be safe and well taken care of. Just be careful and try to bring everyone home."

"Ismail Bay will be watching over him, Constantine. I have given him explicit instructions to watch over your general. I do owe him my life."

George smiled. "Don't worry Mehmet, I am a big boy and can take care of myself."

"I know George but it is always good to have a trusted friend watching you back halfway around the world."

"I will take that under consideration. We will watch each other's back."

"Thank you, General. Try to bring him back in one piece Ismail, he is a good friend. I owe him my kingdom and family."

"Don't worry my padishah I will be back."

"That brought a laugh from the sultan?"

"I see you are learning the Ottoman ways. The young man came over and hugged George. Good luck in the new world my friend. And may Allah watch over you."

"Thank you. I will need it and listen to Julie."

"You can bet on that my friend."

The emperor came over and also gave his friend a hug. "We would all not be here if it were not for you George. May God always watch over you my friend and brother."

"Thanks Constantine."

George turned to leave. "George!" Mary came running over holding her son Justinian and hugged him.

"Thanks sarge for all you did for us. Without you we would have never survived in this world."

"Watch over Anna," he said as he kissed the small child.

"Both Constantine and I will. You are both part of our family," she kissed him on the cheek. "Watch over Constantine too."

Having said his good byes, George turned and headed for his flagship, the Limnos."

Marseilles, France
May23, 1454

After a week of calm sailing the two steam frigates had reached the port of Marseilles. It was still too early to be called the country of France. The hundred year's war had just ended the year before. The city was under the rule of Duke René of Anjou. The two ships dropped anchor a half a mile from the port, the Byzantine ensigns flying prominently, so there would be no mistake to who the ships belonged too. George was hoping they could buy fresh supplies and wood for their boilers before they set out to cross the Atlantic. Lieutenant Commander Green kept the ships at general quarters but had not run the guns out. Hopefully there would be no problems with the locals.

George admired the fortifications that ringed the harbor. They looked almost impregnable at least for armies of that time period. With heavy cannon the fortifications could be eventually be breached but not without heavy loses to any attacker. Several warships were also docked in the harbor, but with the firepower that the two frigates had they would become matchsticks in minutes.

George stood on the bridge with General Ismail Bay and scanned the docks. "We've been here over an hour and no one has come out to greet or threaten us yet."

"You spoke too soon Ismail. Here comes a boat with several officials on it. Let's go greet them. Remember we would like to establish relations with them. It could be a provisioning stop before we cross the Atlantic for future voyages."

Ten minutes later the boat had come alongside the Limnos which had been flying George's pennant. Several high ranking officers came on board. One of them an older officer dressed in highly polished armor approached George and the marine honor guard armed with bayonet tipped Mosin Nagant rifles. "I am Admiral Philippe Lanois, the naval commander here," he said in broken Greek."

"I am Duke George Mavrakis commanding General of this task force. This is General Ismail Bay my second in command. Parlevouz Englais?"

"Yes I do." George figured they would speak some English after fighting the British for the last 100 years.

"We come in friendship and we bring greeting from the emperor of Byzantium and the Ottoman Sultan. We would like to purchase supplies."

"How dare you sail into our port? You will immediately allow my forces to board your ships. You are our prisoners."

"You must be joking admiral. We come in peace and will pay for our supplies in gold."

"You are only two ships I have six galleys they will capture your ships. Surrender peacefully."

"Sir, the warships are pulling out of the docks."

"Run out the guns, commander."

"Aye, Aye, sir." Within 30 seconds all the gun were run out on both frigates."

"Admiral we will blow your ships out of the water and kill innocent men for no reason. This ship does not need the wind to move it. It is powered by steam. You will also be committing an act of war against both the Byzantine and Ottoman Empires. Within a month we will return with many ships and heavy guns and pound your city to rubble and hang its leaders for daring to start an unprovoked war."

"Sir the ships are turning and heading this way."

"Anchor is up and so is steam, sir," Lieutenant Stavrou, the ships executive officer said.

"Commander, do you see that small ship anchored about 300 meters just off our port side?"

"I do, sir."

"It looks empty. Sink it. "

"All ahead slow. Yes, sir."

"Starboard batteries, gun one through six open fire."

Almost in unison six 32 pounder naval cannon opened fire. Four solid shot iron balls hit the small coaster literally smashing it to bits. The Admiral and the rest of his officers were in shock from what they had just witnessed. "Please we've made a terrible mistake."

"Admiral, I strongly suggest you send your men to stop your fleet from being destroyed."

"Yes, yes general I will immediately give the order."

"Helmsman, all stop."

The admiral gave an order in French and the three of his officers quickly climbed down and into the small boat tied along the side that brought them out to the frigates and quickly rowed toward the approaching warships. The small boat pulled up to the first galley and the officers on board. Five minutes later the ships turned around and headed back towards the docks.

"Now admiral, you will allow us to buy the supplies we need. Like I said we will pay in gold and silver. My men will be allowed to come on shore and enjoy themselves we will cause no problems. I warn you though, if anything happens to anyone of my men your fleet will be sunk and your port destroyed. Are we understood?"

"Yes, yes, my apologies this was all a terrible mistake."

"Apologies are accepted, we will no longer discuss this unfortunate mistake. Please have a seat and a glass of wine with me and General Ismail."

"Yes, a glass of wine would be excellent at the moment, said the Admiral Lois still visibly shaken by the demonstration of power of the steam warship."

George escorted the admiral to a table that was set with glasses, a flask of wine and small plates containing meats and cheeses. Let's start from the beginning, admiral. As I said the Emperor of Byzantium and the Ottoman Sultan both send your ruler their greetings. We wish to be friends."

"I will convey this to my sovereign."

"We require some fresh water, fruits, meats vegetables and several tons of cut wood."

"No problem we will sell you anything you need."

"Sir, the small boat is back."

"Admiral would you like a tour of our warship?"

"Why of course, this is a fantastic ship. It could destroy any navy in the world."

"Yes it could. Now gentlemen follow me."

"You have a way with words my friend," General Ismail said with a smile.

*****

A couple of hours later a galley arrived with the admiral and several other officials. George and his staff were invited to the Duke's palace for a banquet. George agreed but he would take two well-armed marine guards along and both he and General Ismail Bay were also both going armed. Colonel Longo was left in command with orders if they did not return by morning, to sink the French ships and blow the harbor and forts to bits. The flagship lowered the Zodiac and transported them to the shore where a carriage and escort were waiting. The French that were waiting in the quay were terrified when they saw the zodiac and the marines dressed in camouflage uniforms and carrying AK47 rifles. It was almost too much for 15th century men to comprehend. Fortunately Admiral Lois was there and kind of knew what to expect from the visitors.

"Hello gentlemen, there is a carriage here to transport you to the castle."

George, Ismail and the two guards climbed aboard and traveled through the town towards the castle. George had not been into any other 15th century European city. Beggars and street urchins were everywhere. He was amazed at the dirt and filth that clogged the streets. The stench of human waste permeated the entire city. He saw people just emptying out the contents of chamber pots from windows and balconies. No wonder disease and the plague were rampant in European cities during this century. Constantinopolis had a sewage system and flushing toilets for the last thousand years. Anna had established a national health department that helped keep the city clean.

When they finally reached the palace the sun had already set. The coach pulled up to the entrance. Lit torches had been placed on the walls to provide light. They were met by the palace guards and were ushered inside. There was no way they could compare this palace with the opulence of the Imperial Palace or the sultan's palace. There they met a middle aged man who introduced himself as Duke René of Anjou. He held out his hand which George shook, the man also spoke passable English and Greek.

"Welcome to Marseilles, Duke Mavrakis."

"Thank you, sir. Both Emperor Constantine and Sultan Mehmet send you their greetings and wish you good health and would like you to have this small gift as a token of our friend ship." George handed the duke a thin three foot wooden box engraved with the Byzantine eagle in gold.

The duke opened the box and pulled out a slim tube. "Thank you. But what is it?"

"It's called a telescope, Duke René. Put it up to your eye and look at the moon or something faraway it will make it look closer."

"Please call me René."

"Call me George, René."

The duke walked to one of the windows put the scope to his eye and peered at the moon. Even though the telescope was only thirty power, it still was able to show the pock marked face of the lunar surface and rings of Saturn. "My god, there are many mountains and holes on the moon and Saturn has a ring around it."

"Yes Saturn does have a ring and there are large mountains on the moon, René. The holes are called craters some of them are tens of leagues across and they were caused by huge rocks called meteors crashing into the moon. One day man will visit the moon. It is a barren place. There is no life there."

"This is an amazing instrument my friend. Thank you."

"You are welcome."

"Please join me at my table my friends."

George and Ismail took seats next to the duke with the two marine guards standing behind them. The table was adorned with roast chicken and wild boar.

"Do you always have body guards along?"

"Not usually but when our initial greeting was less than friendly what is one to think?"

"That was a mistake from an overzealous commander. I apologize for that."

"But you only have two men with you. I have over fifty soldiers here?"

"With the weapons my two men are carrying they could slaughter most of your men before you could finish drinking you glass of wine. Plus we are also carrying weapons that could kill over twenty of your men if we wanted. Besides I have given orders to my executive office to destroy your navy and the port if we do not return by morning."

"The duke stared at George for a moment and there was completes silence."

"The duke smiled. "I would have given the same orders my friend. But you are not even carrying a sword?"

George pulled out his Beretta 9mm pistol. "I have this hand gun."

"May I see it?"

George ejected the round in that was in the chamber took the magazine out and handed the pistol to the duke. "So this gun can fire many times?"

"Yes, it can fire 15 times when fully loaded." George showed a bullet to the duke. This is a bullet it contains the powder and bullet together.

"This is so amazing. The Byzantine empire is producing these weapons?"

"We are producing many types of weapons. We are even producing flying machines that can drop explosives from the sky."

"But how is this possible? Only angles can fly, with the will of god."

"It is called science and technology. We have built great universities to train our best and brightest in science and medicine. We've harnessed steam to propel our ships and our physicians have developed drugs that can cure many sicknesses."

"With these weapons you can conquer the world."

"We don't want to do that, René. We are a peace loving people."

"We heard that you defeated the Ottomans over a year ago in a great siege. Now you have them along as your slaves?"

"No, your eminence. We are equals and allies. After our total defeat the Byzantines showed us mercy and a better way to grow and prosper as a people," General Ismail Bay said."

"That is very noble of your emperor, George, showing an enemy mercy."

"It avoids hatred and prevents future wars."

"That is true. Would you sell us some of these weapons and technology?"

"We may sell some things to our friends. We would like to establish diplomatic relations with you and the French crown. I will also invite you to send ten students to Constantinopolis to study in our university."

"The Ottoman Empire would also host your students in our university."

"Thank you, gentlemen. What do you want in return?"

"All we ask is for your friendship and the ability to use your port as a stop to provision our ships for the voyages across the Atlantic Ocean. It would be mutually beneficial agreement for all."

"But the world is flat the ships will fall off."

"No René, the world is actually round. Its circumference is 24,000 miles. There is a very large continent, about four thousand miles due west from the Pillars of Hercules and we are headed there."

"I envy you, George. You will be going on a voyage of discovery which is fraught with danger. You may find many riches there."

"Yes, we will discover many new things there. Your city and France could benefit and serve as a trading gateway to the rest of Europe.

"Our nation is not united yet. The war with the English just finished. We must rebuild and quit squabbling amongst ourselves."

"You must unite the nation and build a strong France.

"You are correct about that my friend. We would definitely be interested in establishing relations and trade with Byzantium and the Ottoman Empire. We will send a ship to Constantinopolis to establish an embassy."

"Please visit my ship tomorrow and I will give you a letter so your ambassador can present himself to Emperor Constantine."

"Thank you George. I hope our two countries become good friends and business partners. Now please enjoy the food and refreshments."

Straits of Gibraltar
May 28, 1454

The French true to their word had provided the needed supplies for the expedition and were paid in gold. Prior to the ships departure from Marseilles, Duke René Anjou visited the Limnos and received a tour which only reinforced their desire to establish ties with both the Byzantine and Ottoman Empires. Prior to leaving the ship, George showed the duke how to use a Makarov Pistol, than gave him one with 100 rounds and another telescope as a parting gift. This second gift would pay huge dividends in the future. The next day the duke sent a messenger asking for a meeting with Luis XI the dauphine (heir to the throne) of France, advising him of what had transpired, thus setting events into motion that would have geopolitical repercussions.

Three days later, the two frigates were nearing the straits of Gibraltar and the entrance to the broad Atlantic Ocean. George viewed the massive rock through his binoculars that would one day in the future, at least in his past timeline come under British control. If he had anything to do with it, the Byzantines would one day in the near future have to capture the strategic outpost that was now under Moorish control.

"Sails ho." The lookout pointed to the southwest.

George peered through his binoculars and spotted five galleys coming up rapidly from the North African side of the straits.

"Commander Green, Do you see those five pirate galleys they are going to try and cut us off from the strait."

"Green raised his glasses to his eyes. I see them too, sir. Lieutenant Paraskevas, beat to general quarters. Also call the Empress Mary on the radio and have her prepare for combat. We will fight our way through the straights."

"Aye, Aye, sir." The marine drummer began to beat to quarters and the crew hurried to their combat stations. The ships guns were quickly run out and the marines went up to their fighting tops armed with the new percussion rifles. Several of the marine NCOs had been issued with Mosin Nagant sniper rifles to kill enemy officers. The Imperial guards and the Ottoman contingent remained below decks. They would not be needed for this fight.

"All ahead full."

"All ahead full sir," the officer of the bridge verbally acknowledged as he relayed the order down to the engine room through the brass voice tube.

The side paddle wheels began turning and the ship began to

pick up speed. Soon the Limnos was sailing at ten knots followed closely behind by the Empress Mary. The five galleys split into two formations and headed towards the two frigates. Green could see over a hundred armed men in each ship. "Prepare to fire as we bear." With lanyard in their hand the gun captains stood buy to fire their guns.

The first two galleys closed in on the Limnos. Green gave the order to fire when the enemy ships were less than 100 meters distant. "Helmsman, hold her steady. Fire as we bear now!"

The 32 pounders roared to life, each gun firing individually as the target came into range. The 32-pound solid shot crashed into the galleys at point blank range, smashing them to match sticks

"Cease fire!"

When the smoke finally cleared the Limnos had left two sinking wrecks in her wake. There were only a few survivors in the water. The other enemy ships seeing the devastation wrought on the two other galleys quickly turned to run.

"I want these pirates sunk, commander. We don't want them praying on future shipping transiting the straights."

"Good call General Mavrakis. I would leave one survivor so they can go tell their friends to leave ships flying the Byzantine ensign alone."

"That is a good idea General Ismail. Tell the Empress Mary commander, to let the lead ship get away."

"Aye, aye, sir."

Within thirty minutes two of the three pirate ships had been sunk and the two frigates resumed their journey.

CHAPTER 9

Mid Atlantic Ocean
June 25, 1454

It had been almost two and a half weeks since they had left the small Portuguese colony of São Miguel in the Azores. Commander Green had used several charts for navigation that he had brought over with him on his IPAD to find the island. The colony of São Miguel had been settled for less than ten years, there were less than a thousand colonists on the island. After dropping anchor, George and General Ismail had gone to the small settlement of Vila Franca do Campo and met the town leaders. Theirs' was the first ships the inhabitants had seen for a couple of years. The town's people had never heard of Byzantium and were in mesmerized by the ships and gear the visitors had brought with them. After a couple days of shore leave for the crew on the green and temperate island and replenishing their supplies, the two ships headed out into the north Atlantic.

George and the look outs scanned the horizon looking for the first signs of land. Even though they were in hurricane season, the weather remained good and the two frigates made good speed, averaging 8 knots under full sail. Green's home- made barometer, a weather glass displayed high pressure all the way across. (The weather glass is a teapot like container, made of blown glass, with a wide body and a thin spout which is the only opening to the larger part of the weather glass. It is filled with water, preferably colored, to a little above the connection between the body and the spout.

Rising air pressure will push the liquid back down the spout, whereas falling pressure will cause the water to rise in the spout, even to the point where it over flows)

Late yesterday afternoon a pair of seagulls had landed on the ship, land could not be that far off.

"We should be seeing land soon gentlemen. If my navigation is correct we should be about 30 miles off the mouth of the Hudson river."

"It's not the Hudson yet commander."

"We will need to name it, sir."

"I think it should be named in your honor, general. You are commander of this mission."

"Hmmm, the Mavrakis river. It has a good ring to it, General Ismail. Both men laughed.

"It has an excellent harbor and we will claim this land for Byzantium and New Jersey for the Ottoman Empire,' Green said.

"One day a great city will be built on the large island we will soon see, Ismail. Twelve million people will live on the island. On Sept 11, 2001, two very large flying machines each carrying over 150 people and flying at 500 miles an hour will be crashed into two giant structures over 350 meters tall, by Islamic Jihadi fanatics killing 3000 people. These men will be members of a fanatic sect called Wahhabis that began in Saudi Arabia in the 1700s. It was supposed to be a purified form of Islam. They turned out to be the worst murderers. They formed a terrorist group called Al Qaeda that will murder both Christians and Muslims that don't believe in their there warped way of Islam. The western world fought back and we were in a never ending war. This is why were in Afghanistan."

"They are an abomination to Islam and everything the Prophet stood for. They should never be allowed to exist."

"Hopefully your sultan lays the ground work to ensure these groups are never allowed to exist but that will be difficult. No one can tell what the new future will bring forth."

"Land ho."

George put his glasses to his eyes and looked towards the west. "There is the new world."

He gave his glasses to General Ismail. "Yes I see the land mass."

*****

By late afternoon the two warships dropped anchor in the newly discovered Mavrakis River, off what would be Battery Park in the future. George gave the order to post guards to deter any unwelcome visitors from the shore. He was sure they had been seen sailing up the river by the natives. In the early morning, both ships sent out longboats to catch the numerous fish that swam in the river and landed foraging parties for hunting and replenishing their fresh water supply. George, Colonel Longo, General Ismail Bay and Colonel Ali Pasha where part of the first group that landed along with a priest and Imam. Both clergy men held a short service on the beach thanking god for their safe arrival in the new world.

"Well gentlemen, we did it. We are in the new world. It is beautiful."

"Yes we did, Colonel Longo. Do you see that small island over there?"

"Yes, sir."

"That will be called Liberty Island. In the 1880s the French will give the United States a very large bronze statue which will be set up there. It will be the first thing millions of immigrants see to include over a million Italians, when the reach the new world for a new life."

"You know we are being watched."

"Yes, I've noticed. I have given our men an order not to fire unless attacked. We don't want to start on the wrong foot. They will make contact with us soon. They are just checking us out. We still have 2000 miles to travel before we reach Mexico. We don't want to start fighting the natives if we can avoid it."

"Sir, look!" Colonel Ali Pasha said pointing at a group of natives that came through the trees carrying baskets.

"Okay everyone don't make any sudden moves. They are coming in in peace and bringing us gifts."

"They look reddish, and have Turkic features," Ismail said.

"We called them redskins in my timeline. It was a derogatory term because of the reddishness of their skin. They came over from Asia walking across the land bridge between North America during the time of the great freeze almost 20,000 years ago. The sea was much smaller snd shallower alonmg the coasts because a lot of water was frozen in ice. So genetically Turks maybe related to some degree."

A group of ten semi clad young native maidens each carrying a basket filled with fish, potatoes, apples and other vegetables accompanied by a dozen male warriors armed with sharp stone hatchets and stone tipped spears walked towards them. George walked towards the group and raised his hand. "Hello." He lightly thumped his chest, "George."

The older native thumped his chest, "Aneme."

George pointed at the man, "Aneme."

The native shook his head, "Aneme," and smiled. The man pointed to the gifts and said something in his language. George took out a silver Byzantine coin with the head of Emperor Constantine on it and gave it to the man. The man looked at the coin shook his head up and down smiled and gave it to one of the other men to hold.

"Colonel Longo, please hand me your knife we will give it as a gift to the chief here. We have many extras on the ship. Besides we will be back one day and may be settling here it is a very strategic part of the continent."

Longo handed the small blade to the native chief saying, "knife."

The man took the blade and ran it on his arm making a small cut. The man yelled and jumped up shaking his head. "Knife, knife!"

"I guess he likes his gift, gentlemen. George pointed to the food and said knife. The chief bobbed his head, "Knife, knife."

"We have some more trinkets for the natives on the ships, sir."

"Let's provision the ship, cut some wood for our boilers and head south, we still got a long way to go."

Gulf of Mexico
July 13, 1454

After giving the men a few of days of shore rest and after provisioning the ships with food and fresh water, they left their anchorage of what would be New York City, and headed south along the east coast of the future united states. The local natives had proven to be friendly and had held a couple of feasts for their visitors whom they considered gods. George was sure that nine months from now there would be several half native Greek or Turkish children running around. The sailing and wind conditions were good and they only had to run the engines for a couple of days.

Within six days they had dropped anchor in the St Johns River in a sheltered anchorage of what would one day be Mayport Naval Base in the city of Jacksonville Florida and claimed the area for the Byzantine and Ottoman empires. George sent several boatloads of men ashore and refilled both ships bunkers with cordwood and refilled the fresh water casks. Hurricane season would last till the end of November, there was no way George wanted to be caught short of fuel, in case they head out to sea to ride out a serious storm.

After a long and arduous journey down the coast of Florida and across the Gulf of Mexico the two frigates were nearing the coast of the future state of Texas. It was almost sunrise the first rays of light were beginning to shine in the eastern horizon. George was standing the ship's radio room. He had received reports from the radio operators that they had heard strange voices come from the radio. During the voyage they had attempted to stay in communication with Constantinoplis and Konya as much as possible with the shortwave radio. For the last few days George had given orders not to transmit but to just listen. So far they heard nothing but static coming from the radio. There was no way anyone else could be transmitting in 1454. It was probably interference from the ionosphere.

"Nothing sir. I have not heard anything for the radio for the last three days," Warrant officer Spiros Makris said.

"Maybe it was nothing Spiro. It could have been just interference from the atmosphere."

"I know what I heard, sir. It was a few words in a strange language I never heard before."

The radio cracked with static. "It's been doing that all night, general."

"Wait, do you hear that? There it is, sir?"

George heard it too but the static was too loud he could not understand anything. Then he heard one word, "da." At least that's what he thought he had heard. Then the radio went dead.

"You heard it, sir."

"Yes I think did, Spiro."

"Land ho." George put his glasses to his eyes and looked toward the west. The sun had finally risen over the waters of the gulf. He could see a dark smudge which was land.

"Have a good morning, Spiros."

"Thank you, sir. I' am going to try and get a few hours sleep."

George proceeded up to the bridge where Commander Green was checking his navigation coordinates. "We're near the Texas-Mexico border, sir. Just northeast of the future city of Brownsville."

"Good morning gentlemen," General Ismail Bay said as he walked on to the bridge with a coffee cup in his hand. Both Ottoman and Byzantine traders had recently established trade routes to Ethiopia and had begun coffee importation to Asia Minor.

"Good morning, Ismail."

"We should be dropping anchor by noon. I've ordered us and the Empress Mary to light the boilers build up a head of steam. I want to come in with power."

"That's very wise precaution; we don't know how the currents are around here."

"We may want to set up an outpost here, sir. It's 600 miles to Vera Cruz and 200 miles to Mexico City."

"That is also a good suggestion, commander. You know that Spiro said he was hearing strange voices from the radio?"

"Yeah I heard about it."

"Well, I think I heard them too, just before I came up to the bridge."

"What exactly did you hear, sir?"

"I am not really sure, the static was very bad but I did hear something that sounded like da."

"What is da?"

"It means yes in Russian, Ismail."

"What? That's impossible. Maybe you thought you heard it."

"I agree with General Ismail, sir. You did say the static was very bad."

"Yes, maybe I did. In fact I hope I imagined it. Think about it though. It was the Soviets that were experimenting in time travel and we did come to this time by turning on the equipment on their base. What if they also used it before us?"

"You do bring out a very good point, sir. It is very possible that they may have indeed used the equipment we found in the mine and traveled back in time way before we did."

"We can't take the chance that I imagined what I heard and be caught by surprise. We need to be alert at all times. We will send out patrols to scout the perimeter we set up for at least 25 miles around in all directions."

"General Mavrakis is correct we must take precautions and use the radio sparingly. If we heard them they must have also heard us and know someone else is here."

"They probably have also heard something on their sets but hopefully none of them understand Greek or Turkish, the languages we have been using to talk to our home bases."

"If by any chance the Russians are here, we don't know what they have brought with them and how long they have been here. They could have emerged through a worm hole weeks, months or years ago. If it was the later, they could have built up a significant civil and military infrastructure."

"But they would have travelled back in time over 28 years ago, sometime around 1988 shortly before they pulled out of Afghanistan."

"They may have left their time in 1988 but they could have arrived last year or yesterday. Some could still be travelling in time and arrive next year, sir."

"Now come to think of it, that is true."

"It could even be the Russian Federation. They must have records of their experiments."

"That is possible commander but they would need a unique place like the Iron mountain mine we found in Afghanistan."

"True sir but I'm sure they have hundreds of mines in Siberia a region teeming with untapped resources. Also their time travel technology has advanced leaps and bounds in the 30 years that have passed."

"That's very true. We need to limit our transmissions to once a week and make them quick."

"I agree, commander."

Two hours later both frigates dropped anchor off the mouth of the Rio Grande River on the Texas Mexican border. They had finally arrived at their destination.

Texas-Mexican Border outpost
July 28, 1454

After two weeks of hard work, they had built a fort stockade and several barracks for the troops to live in. Everyone had been happy to finally get off the boat and stretch their legs. Wild game and fish were plentiful. The men hunted and fished and everyone ate well. After a couple of days on shore, they had made contact with the local natives and traded with them for corn, tomatoes, seeds and other vegetables. They even employed several to help with the cutting and building. Some of the natives were already beginning to learn Greek and some of the soldiers were learning native words. Eventually they would have their own vegetable gardens with the seeds they planted. What surprised everyone was the amount of gold jewelry that some of the native locals wore. George figured once they traveled further south they would make contact with the native tribes that inhabited Mexico's interior and were much wealthier that the natives they had so far met.

By the third week, the cavalry scouts had branched out approximately 25 miles in each direction and had only found a couple of native villages, but nothing else of particular interest. When they entered the villages and the natives saw the men on the horses they fell to the ground. Having never seen horses before they thought they were gods. Having established an outpost it was time they moved further on into the interior. The plan was to land in the vicinity of Veracruz and March to Mexico City to visit the Aztec empire. Then one morning everything changed when a native arrived wanting to trade food and gold jewelry. What caught he Turkish Sergeant's eye was the piece of brass the man was wearing around his neck. He brought the man to the attention of George and Colonel Ali Pasha who were inspecting some of the defense works.

"Sirs, I have something to show you that this man was wearing."

"What is it, Sergeant Ahmet?"

He showed them the brass casing that the man had been wearing tied with a leather strand around his neck. George was in complete shock. "Are you okay, sir?"

"Yes, yes, I was just surprised me for a moment. Wow truly, this is unbelievable. A 7.62mm, AK47 shell casing showing up in North America in 1454."

Colonel Ali looked at it too. "Yes you are right, sir. Where could this man have gotten it?"

George sent for one of the native workers that had learned some Greek. His had been given the nick name of Stavros from some of the men. When the man arrived George showed him the casing and asked him to find out where it came from. "What is he saying Stavros?"

"Far from here."

The man pointed towards the interior of the country. "How far?"

The interpreter said something and the other man picked up a stick and he drew mountains. The he pointed to a flag and drew a hammer and a sickle. George shook his head up and down and smiled at the man. The man smiled back.

"We gentlemen, have a serious problem. The Soviets are here."

General Mavrakis immediately called a staff meeting to discuss the new threat and their next move. "Gentlemen we are not here alone. It seems that others have traveled here from my timeline. I guess it should not really be a surprise since the Soviets were the ones that had experimented with time travel."

"Tell us about these Soviets?"

"They were an evil empire that followed a political idea that the government would own everything and the working people would benefit from this and all men would be equal. It was supposed to be a worker's paradise."

"That is not all bad."

"No General Ismail it's not a bad thing in theory. But it never materialized after their bloody revolution into a worker's paradise. It was more of a worker's hell. They were a brutal regime that did not tolerate opposition. They did not believe in any god and murdered millions of their own people. After the second Great War they ended up occupying all of Eastern Europe. We were allies with them to defeat another evil empire created by the Germans. Unfortunately, whatever lands the Soviets liberated from the Germans, they decided to keep. The Soviets eventually built a great military machine but fortunately it was never used. They collapsed in 1990 from lack of an economy and spending all their money on military equipment."

"So if we run it to them they may be hostile?

"I would say yes, Colonel Longo. I would think they would want to be the only strong guys in town and would eliminate any competition."

"So we need to be careful and try to avoid contact?"

"We should avoid direct contact, General Ismail, but we need to find out what they are doing. We can't afford to be caught by surprise. Sooner or later they will build ships and visit Europe."

"If they have brought modern equipment with them they can conquer all of Europe and us to."

"That is true Colonel Ali. If they have been here many years and have native allies they may have already built a fleet that can cross the ocean and can attack at any time. That is why we must find out where they are and what they have brought with them.

Then we load the ships with goods, supplies and water and get back home with the info so we can plan accordingly. Does everyone agree?"

Everyone shook their head agreeing. "Maybe they don't know we are here," Colonel Longo commented.

"We heard them talking on the radio and I am sure they probably heard us too. If they haven't heard us how long do you think it will be before some native tells them about us or the Russians see the knives and other goods we have been trading?"

"I'm sure they would be pretty interested to find out where those goods came from since they know that no Europeans show up her for another 50 years."

"Your are right, General Ismail. And when they do we are in trouble."

"So what do you suggest we do General Mavrakis?"

"I think we need to send a couple of teams into the interior and down the coast to find out just what our Russian friends are doing here."

"Why down the coast?" Colonel Ali asked.

"Because colonel, they must have a naval base on the Atlantic coast if they are planning to eventually expand to Europe."

"You do make a point, sir. They will need ships."

"So what are you planning, general?"?

"We take two groups of fifteen men sail south three hundred miles and land them then sail back north. One of the groups will have a long boat with sails to scour the coast. And look for a naval base. We return in three weeks to pick them up."

"Who will command these two groups?"

Colonel Longo and Colonel Ali Pasha will command them. They are trained and very capable officers."

"I am honored," Colonel Ali said.

"As I too," Longo added.

"It will not be a walk in the Garden, gentlemen. You will be operating in unknown territory with potential enemy everywhere. You will have limited supplies and have to live off the land. You can't afford to be seen by the locals who may report you to the Soviets."

"That's why we have several crossbows with us, sir. We can hunt silently and if we have to kill silently," Longo said.

"Same here, sir."

"Gentlemen, choose your men and begin preparations we leave in a week. I want an equal mix of Byzantine and Ottoman troops. Longo you will have the interior to check and Ali will have the coast. In the mean time I want a ship patrolling the southern quadrant at all times and the remaining ship to have steam up each morning and look outs posted at te entrance of the bay. Commander, please arrange that."

"Will do, sir."

"General, please ensure we have guards and patrols posted at all times. I do not want us to get caught here with our pants down."

"Understood, sir."

Constantinopolis
July 29, 1454

The emergency meeting of the Byzantine Security Council had been requested by Emperor Constantine. The morning meeting had been called at the new military headquarters adjacent at the palace. Present were the Ottoman ambassador and Military Attaché Brigadier General Osman Karras. For the Byzantines General Notaras the head of the Joint Chiefs of chief of staff, Major Jenkins the acting military security advisor and several other staff officers were present. The emperor walked in and everyone stood up in respect to the Byzantine leader and military commander and chief.

"Please gentlemen take your seats and enjoy the coffee and pastries. I hope you all enjoy the Ethiopian coffee. I have developed a particular liking to it. How about you General Karras?"

"It is very good your majesty. It has made its way to Konya. Especially know that we control Egypt and the Red Sea ports."

"It is one positive thing that our American friends showed us. Now I've called you here for more than coffee. We received a communication from our new world expedition yesterday. It seems they have been picking up other voices on their radios."

"What? Other voices?" The Ottoman military Attaché Asked.

"It gets even better. A local native came in wearing a brass bullet casing around his neck." Constantine pulled one out of his pocket and held it up for all to see. "It similar to this, a 7.62mm brass bullet casing. Ammunition used for the Russian AK-47 assault rifles."

"May Allah protect us all the," said General Karras.

"When we had one of the natives that learned some Greek ask the man where he found it he pointed towards the interior of the continent. When they asked them who he got I from he pointed at the Byzantine and Ottoman flags and drew a hammer and a sickle with a stick in the dirt."

"Holly shit! We are not alone."

"No you are not Major Jenkins it seems the Soviets are here too."

"Who are these Soviets?

"Major Jenkins, would you please explain to the general who the Soviets are."

"In short it was a Marxist–Leninist state on the Eurasian continent that existed between 1922 and 1991. It was governed as a single-party state by the Communist Party with Moscow as its capital. Marxism and Leninism was a political philosophy developed in the late 1800s by Karl Marx. Marxism envisioned a philosophy that after a revolution of the workers, the state would take over all property and the means of production and create a workers paradise.

In 1917 after fairing badly fighting Germany in the first Great War and losing millions of soldiers, there was a revolution in Russia that overthrew the Czar. Within a year another revolution by the Marxists overthrew the democratic government, killed the Czar and his family and created a communist dictatorship which became the Soviet Union. They killed millions of their own people. We allied with the Soviets in the 2nd world war in 1941 to defeat a worse menace, Nazi Germany. The Soviets lost over 25 million people in the war. Their armies liberated Eastern Europe which they made part of their empire. They built a great military machine at the expense of their economy which they could have used to eventually conquer all of Europe but we never fought them. Thank god. The world would have been destroyed because between them and the United States we had tens of thousands of nuclear weapons that would have destroyed most of life on earth. The fear of each of us destroying each other (MAD) mutual assured destruction prevented a 3rd and final world war.

In 1979 they invaded Afghanistan to help a communist regime there. They fought the Jihadists to a standstill and finally pulled out in 1988. They collapsed in 1991 and most of the nations they occupied, became democratic states. When we were trapped in the mine shaft after the Taliban suicide bomber blew himself up we went in deeper and found the underground Soviet base. We turned on the power and got transported here. Now it seems we were not the only ones. They Soviets are here to."

"So how long have they been here?"

"We don't know ambassador. It could be 20 years or 20 months. When one travels in time they could show up anywhere and at any time. They may still have people traveling and show up years from now."

"So will these Soviets be friendly or hostile?"

"They were never known as being the friendliest people around. They believed in power and domination. If they are here they will want to be the only power around, subjugate the rest and create a Soviet Utopia here."

"Thank you, Major Jenkins."

"I'm glad to be of service, your majesty."

"It now seems we have a serious problem."

"Yes, General Karras, it seems we do. We don't know how many came over and how long they have been here. General Mavrakis is preparing to send out a mission to find and evaluate the Russian threat."

"We will need to prepare our forces to fight them jointly so we can hit them hard. If we don't they will defeat us piecemeal. If the Russians know about us they will want to destroy us before we get too strong."

"Yes that is a valid point since we don't know what they have brought with them."

"Fortunately they are on the other side of the world and it will take very large ships to transport any fighting vehicles they could have brought along," General Notaras added.

"Thank god for that."

"Maybe we can get the other European powers to ally with us, your majesty?"

"Possibly the French Mr. Ambassador, but otherwise most of the other European powers are jealous fools, which most likely ally with the Russians to destroy us instead."

"You make a good point, sir. First of all Venice!"

"Now I do have some good news, our miners were finally able to clear out the tons of rubble that were blocking it and open up the new mine shaft we found. The shaft is huge and it leads into another large gallery filled with all sorts of equipment."

"What new surprises were in it that will make Byzantium even stronger?"

"Now ambassador we have been sharing with you in our discoveries. In light of the new threat we will now share much more with you."

"You have been very generous with us your majesty. I must apologize for my unwarranted remark."

"Never mind Mr. Ambassador. Major Jenkins, will you please highlight what we have found so far."

"Thank you, your majesty. It took us almost two months of around the clock digging to clear the hundreds of tons of debris blocking the tunnel the entrance. It looks like it was blocked intentionally with explosives. When we finally entered we found a treasure trove of equipment. There were crates of AK47s, pistols, light and heavy machine guns and tens of thousands of rounds of ammo for them. We found several light mortars with hundreds of rounds and cases of RPGs lining the tunnel walls. When we entered the main gallery we found two trucks loaded with plastic explosives, radios, binoculars a couple of field guns and ammo and several portable gas generators to include other miscellaneous stuff like drills pumps, miles of wire and cabling, medical and scientific equipment. Behind the trucks were two T-72 main battle tanks with crates of ammo for them."

"What is a T-72 tank? Is it like the metal monster you used to defeat us with?"

"It's much more powerful. The T-72 is a very heavy metal fighting vehicle weighing 20 thousand kilos with a very large 125mm canon that is able to destroy other tanks from long distances. The tanks need to be put back into working order after not moving for over 28 years."

"Will the Ottomans get one?"

"We can train a crew but it is too heavy to transport and needs diesel fuel to run. We now are allies, we would never use these against you," Ambassador! "Replied the emperor.

"Please continue, major."

"We also found three crated Polikarpov, Po-2 biplanes, with several spare motors and parts. Additionally, we found sealed underground tanks holding at least a million liters of diesel and tens of thousands of gallons of gasoline and avgas. There are also rooms filled with lathes, generators, reloading equipment and other valuable equipment We also found tools, crated engines, gas powered drilling equipment that can be used for oil or water drilling. We also found a library of chemistry, metal working and engineering books on how to build steam engines, gas engines and generators. Most are in Russian, we found a couple in English. There are many other items such as wire, magnets and other items to create a power station. That's mostly it your majesty."

"Tell them about the special weapon you discovered, major."

"Are you sure, your majesty?"

"If we are now to fight for our survival we must have full disclosure, major."

"Yes, your majesty.

"When I was searching the gallery I found a locked room. We had to cut the luck off with a special metal cutting torch. When I entered the room I found a small device with radioactive markings making me believe it is a small nuclear weapon maybe 10-100 kiloton. I am not a nuclear weapons technician."

"What is a nuclear weapon?" General Karras asked.

"During out last great world war that was fought from 1939 to 1945, we were able to develop a super weapon called an atomic bomb. This weapon harnessed the building blocks of the universe to create an explosion. It harnesses the power of what makes the sun work. It would take us maybe several air raids with a thousand flying machines to destroy a city, now with one single flying machine and one of these bombs we could destroy an entire city."

"With one bomb you can destroy an entire city?"

"Yes, sir. We dropped one on the Japanese city of Hiroshima it had the power of 15 thousand tons of explosives and it destroyed the city and killed over 80 thousand people."

"In the name of Allah, this is a horrible weapon."

"Yes sir, it is a horrible weapon because it also poisons the ground, air and the people in the area where it detonates for many many years. Many die from this poison called radiation, years later. We dropped a second on the City of Nagasaki killing the same amount of people. After this the Japanese surrendered to us. It is a terrible weapon and we had built thousands of them.

Some of them many hundreds of times more powerful than the Hiroshima bomb. We mounted them on rockets that could hit any area on the earth in 30 minutes. Man had the power to destroy the world."

"It is a terrible weapon, but it may prove useful against the Soviets if we can figure out how to use it and deliver it. It is presently under heavy guard," General Notaras said.

"Now we wait till we hear what our people in the new world find out. I have a feeling that this will not turn out very well and we will have to tool up for a long protracted war that will tax our people and resources and even threaten our survival as free people."

"I will have to immediately inform Konya."

"This is top secret information ambassador. It's only for the Sultan's ears. I may fly down there to meet with the sultan once we find out more. In the mean time we will wait for more news and plan accordingly."

CHAPTER 10

East coast of Mexico
August 6, 1454

It would soon be sunrise in the warm waters of the Gulf of Mexico. The Steam frigate Limnos was steaming at a sedate 8 knots due south, hugging the Mexican coastline. She had been heading south for two days towards Veracruz. Except for a few native fishing boats they had seen no sign of the Soviets. The Limnos was carrying the two commando teams that would be scouting for the Russian presence on the continent. General George Mavrakis was also on the bridge. This mission would be crucial for their survival and their nation's survival. "Sir we are about 150 miles north of Veracruz. If I was the Soviets, that's where I would build a naval base. It's a straight shot of a few hundred kilometers to Mexico city."

"I agree, commander. This is far enough then. I don't want to get seen by any Russian patrols."

"All stop! Drop the anchor, lieutenant."

"Aye, aye commander."

The Limnos came to a full stop about a mile from the shore. "Have all look outs posted lieutenant, we don't need any surprises."

"Aye, aye, sir."

"Commander, please have both Colonel Longo and Ali report to the bridge. Prepare the longboat for launching."

"Yes, sir."

Ten minutes later both officers had arrived on the bridge and were meeting with General Mavrakis. "Good morning gentlemen, are you and your teams ready to put all the training you did to the test?"

"Yes we are sir," Colonel Ali Pasha answered.

"My team is also ready to go, sir."

"You will have the hardest task to accomplish, Colonel Longo. You will have to make your way in land and survive off the land and not get detected. I am also giving you Stavros to act as an interpreter; his Greek has really been improving."

"Thanks sir, we may need him. We'll be careful and manage just fine."

"Colonel Ali we will be dropping you off with the longboat find their naval base but don't get detected. We are giving you a PK machine gun with several thousand rounds and a couple of RPGs. You will also have a 75hp out board engine and a canister of gasoline that you can use in an emergency. It should give you at least 15mph if you need to get away fast. You also have Lieutenant Davis with you. Please bring him back in one piece."

"We too will be ok, sir. Thanks for the motor. I hope we never have to use it. We can supplement our food with fish. The waters here are filled with fish. We brought a net along and fishing equipment. I promise to bring the lieutenant back in one piece."

"We will be return here in two weeks to pick you up. We will wait for two days. Be careful don't get discovered by the Soviets if you can help it. May god be with you." With that the two officers went back to their men and prepared to leave the ship.

Colonel Longo and his team were transported to shore, while Colonel Ali and his men boarded the long boat raised the sail and headed south. The Limnos raised her anchor and headed back to her base, several hundred miles to the north.

Coast of Veracruz, Mexico
August 10, 1454

For the last four days Colonel Ali and his team slowly sailed south checking all the bays and inlets for signs of the Soviets. On the evening of the fourth day while sailing about a mile offshore, Lieutenant Davis noticed a smudge on the south western horizon. Ten minutes later he gave the glasses to Colonel "Sir I see a sail on the horizon."

"I see it too. Looks like a large ship."

He handed the glasses back to the lieutenant. "Drop the sail and quickly row for the shore. We can't be seen by them."

The sail was quickly lowered and three sets of oars were put out. The long boat quickly picked up speed. "I see gun ports and three masts, sir. She seems to be the size of a large frigate."

"She is turning this way. I hope we weren't seen by them. She is also flying a Soviet flag sir."

Within ten minutes the longboat reached the mangroves by the shore and hid among them the numerous channels. Forty-five minutes later the frigate had come into view. She was about a mile off shore and had dropped her sails. "Shit, shit, shit!"

"What is it Lieutenant?"

Davis hand the binoculars to Colonel Ali. "Look behind her."

"I see bubbling behind her and a smoke stack. That is strange, no paddles on her sides?"

"She is a screw frigate, sir. She has a propeller behind her; she is larger, probably faster and more maneuverable than our ships. They are a generation ahead of us in sea power, colonel."

"We need to find their base and get the information back to

our people."

"Seems we found the Russians or the Russians found us."

Soviet Frigate Azov
August 10, 1454

The Soviet 50 gun 2200 ton Steam screw frigate Azov was now only a half mile from the shore and the water was quickly becoming shallower inder her keel. Captain Yuri Petrovich stood on the bridge checking the coastline through his binoculars. The lookout was positive he had spotted a small sailing craft near the shore. Whomever or whatever it was, had disappeared.

"Sir we only have three fathoms and will run aground if we get any closer said the ship's executive officer."

"Dead slow. Do not get any closer to the shore commander."

"Aye, aye, sir."

The steam frigate Azov had been sent north to patrol the coast after strange voices were heard on the shortwave radio. It was the first time since their arrival through the time portal five years earlier, that anything besides Russian voices were heard on the radio. If the voices were real then someone else had mastered time travel. He himself had not heard anything but others allegedly had. He had volunteered along with 1000 other men and women, to travel back in time to establish a socialist empire that would rule the world. Yuri graduated the N. G. Kuznetsov Naval Academy with a physics and naval engineering degree. When he had reached the rank of commander he had gone back to school and received a Master degree in chemistry. Afterwards Yuri had been appointed as chief engineer and nuclear propulsion officer on the Kirov battle cruiser with the northern fleet. When the a message arrived seeking volunteers in the ranks of petty officer to Captain with sailing experience for a special mission, he had been one of the first to volunteer. Another requirement in the message was that the volunteers should be single or have a family with children no younger than ten. Having no family ties and years of sailboat experience, he volunteered for the special mission.

During the initial interview he had been told that mission would take him away from Russia for many years in very difficult conditions. After going through days of medical tests and being questioned by psychiatrists, he was told that he had passed all the medical and psychological tests. He and the other naval volunteers that had been selected were given a crash course in sailing and captaining the large four mast naval academy tall ship, the Kruzenshtern. After mastering the technique of captaining a large sailing ship they were given artillery lessons in 19th century naval cannon. This was all very strange why would they want them learning about 19th century sailing ships and guns? What was even stranger was that the army officers were selected on their knowledge of 18th and 19th century warfare and weaponry. Finally they were all taken to a secret army base in Kazakhstan close to the Afghan border and put into a large auditorium. A senior officer walked on to the stage and introduced himself as General Vladimir Balkov the mission commander. He told them that they Soviet Union was collapsing, the capitalist had finally broken them economically, but all was not lost. Soviet science had found way to save the revolution. An underground base had been built in Afghanistan, where they would all be transported back in time to alter history and begin the people's revolution much earlier. This is why everyone needed special skills to be able to survive in the past. Yuri though the man was crazy and this was all a joke. Well the joke had been on him.

They all had arrived in the Americas before its colonization and according to the scientist who looked at the star coordinates, the year was 1445. They had not expected to go so far back in time they scientist said they would travel anywhere between 300 to 500 years, but it could have been worse. Fortunately they had planned well and included scientists, engineers, miners, chemists, doctors and all those needed to start a new society and brought along enough materials and supplies for the task. The first couple of years had been difficult but with the help of thousands of slaves the Aztecs had provided, they were able to build the infrastructure needed to move forward. According to the scientists they were technologically in level with the 1850s in their old time line. Within a few years they would reach the early 1900s. He was tired dealing with these savages and wished he was back at home in civilization. Unfortunately that was not possible and if one complained to hard they were deemed a counter revolutionary and handed over to the Aztecs for sacrifice to their gods.

"Sir, none of the lookouts report anything. They may be hiding in the mangroves."

"That is if they saw anything to begin with."

"Sir, both lookouts swear they saw a small sailing craft."

"Maybe it was the local natives fishing?"

"It's possible but that sailing rig was not common to the natives according to the lookouts. The sails looked like they were canvas not thatched."

"Thank you, commander."

He wished he had radar unit installed. Even the small units that they had brought along would have worked just fine. Except for the one installed on the flagship the Kirov which was only run at night for navigation, no one had seen a need to install them since they had arrived in North America and Columbus needed another 50 years to discover the place.

"Sir, do you want us to search the mangroves?"

"No, it will be getting dark soon. We can give our gunners some practice it has been a while. I want you to fire a couple of broadsides into the mangroves."

"Yes sir. Lieutenant, call everyone to general quarters."

Lieutenant Davis was watching the Russian frigate as it sailed closer. He noticed the ship turn and open its gun ports. He screamed a warning. "Sir, they've opened their gun ports they are going to fire on the shore. I suggest we take cover in the water under the boat."

"Do it now."

"Everyone in the water under the boat now!"

Just as the last man got in the water the frigate fired from about a half mile off shore. Several heavy 32lb solid shots crashed into the nearby mangroves sending splinters flying everywhere, several striking the long boat. After a few seconds everyone raised their heads. The frigate had turned around and was heading back up the shore and fired again this time the broadside landed several hundred yards from their location.

"I think that's it. We can get back into the boat."

Everyone quickly climbed in and noticed the damage the broadside had done to the mangroves. Luckily they had been hiding behind several trees. "Had we been in the boat some of us would have been killed or injured horribly, colonel. They weren't just randomly shooting; they must have seen us or thought they had seen something. It's getting later or they would more than likely sent boats to search the mangroves. We were lucky in more ways than one."

"The prophet was looking over all of us, today. Look at all the splinters. Your timely warning saved us, lieutenant. We must be more careful. Let's find a place to camp and call it a day."

Interior of Vera Cruz
August 12, 1454

For almost a week Longo and his team had been trudging into the Mexican interior. Game was plentiful so food was not a problem. They had run into many natives of Mayan stock and they traded small items or food and information. It was not until they reached a small native village containing about 30 adobe structures about 100 kilometers in the interior that they had their first run in with an Aztec patrol.

The thirteen-man team had camped in a clump of trees for the night overlooking the village. The next morning, they were awakened by screams and gunfire. Lieutenant Kemal Aturk who was taking the early morning watch grabbed his glasses and peered towards the village. He was immediately joined by Colonel Longo. "What do you see Kemal?"

"I count twenty men wearing uniforms, two of them have feather headdresses probably officers. The soldiers are carrying what looks to be flintlock muskets."

"What are they doing, Lieutenant?"

"It looks like they are rounding up people, sir. Here take a look."

Longo watched as they went from house to house rounding up people and putting them in chains. He saw a man run out of a house and head toward the tree line but one of the guards raised his musket and shot him. The soldier walked up to the man and plunged his bayonet into him insuring he was dead. The dead man's wife came out of the house and began to wail. "My god they just killed a man. Here take the glasses, Kemal; I'm going to get mine."

A couple of minutes later Longo returned with the rest of the team. "What have they been doing lieutenant?"

"It looks like they are collecting people and putting them in chains, colonel. If I had to guess this is a slave collecting expedition."

"Slaves, for whom?" The locals according to General Mavrakis were not supposed to have metal?"

"Those guys maybe are Aztec warriors that General Mavrakis had told us about. They had conquered and enslaved the entire region. They must be collecting the prisoners for the Russians. If they have metal chains with them, they could have only gotten them from the Russians because the Aztecs had never prouced iron."

Longo handed the binoculars to Stavros their native interpreter. Who are the soldiers with the guns?"

"Aztecs, they very bad people! They take workers for Russians."

"Maybe we should help these people out. They may tell us what's going on and where the Russians are."

"That is a good idea, sir. It may even endear us to the natives."

"Let's set up a plan. We want to hit them when they leave the village and are out in the open. They have only flintlock muskets so we should be able to pick them off at a distance."

After another forty five minutes of mayhem the Aztecs had rounded up about thirty prisoners, twenty five men and five women. They were chained to one another and with the crack of a whip they were herded out of the village towards the west. For most of the morning the commando team worked their way past the Aztecs and reached a forested area where the Aztecs would have to pass with their prisoners.

Longo gathered the team around him. "This is a great place for an ambush. We'll take them out here. After I fire the first shot open up and take them out."

Having briefed the team he gave the order to take their positions for the ambush. Everyone quickly took their spot and waited. Within ten minutes the Aztecs with their prisoners had reached the ambush position. At head of the column was an officer with five soldiers. Longo flipped the selector level on auto, jumped out of the bush and fired a controlled burst at the six men instantly cutting them down. Before the Aztecs could take any action the rest of Longo's team opened fire. Most of the guards did not even have a chance to fire off a shot before being cut down by accurate AK 47 fire. Two of the guards in the rear one of them an officer had fired off their muskets and pulled out their swords and stood waiting. "Cease fire! These two are mine."

Lieutenant Aturk a former officer of the elite Janissary corps o took the challenge, pulled out his sword, an Ottoman Scimitar and charged the two men. The first Aztec a soldier swung his sword at the lieutenant. Aturk ducked and with a single swipe almost took the man's head off. The Aztec officer took the opportunity and charged. Aturk side stepped and the charging Aztec went past him. Before the Aztec could recover Aturk ran him through.

In less than a minute the ambush was over, the twenty Aztec soldiers were either lying dead or dying as was one of the prisoners who had been shot by a guard after attacking him. Almost immediately the chained prisoners picked up stones and crushed the skills of all the guards that still gave a sign of life. One of the prisoners got the keys from the dead guards and unlocked the chains. When they saw Longo and his team they dropped to the ground in fear. Longo motioned to the interpreter. "Ask them who were these men and where were they being taken."

The rest of the team had gathered around as interpreter spoke to the Natives for a couple of minutes then he translated what they said. "The soldiers are Aztecs allies of the Soviets. They collect people to work in factories, farms and mines."

"Where were they taking them?"

"To Soviets."

"How far are they from here?"

Their native interpreter asked the former prisoners and they replied that the Soviets were located in large compound which could be reached by sundown.

"Ask them if someone could take us there?"

Stavros asked the freed prisoners and one of the younger men agreed to take them to the Soviet base.

"Before we leave collect all the bodies and bury them. We don't want anyone to find them and see that they were killed by modern fire arms. Afterwards we can go find the Soviets."

East Coast of Mexico
August 13, 1454

Have sailed a couple of days further south along the coast, Colonel Ali and his team began seeing more evidence of Soviet influence. They had even discovered a Native village that had mostly likely been attacked and destroyed by the Soviets, having found AK47 shell casings on the ground. It was on the afternoon of the second day that they had observed several sailing vessels making their way up the coast, that Ali decided to beach the boat and head south by foot. By late evening they had reached an outcrop that overlooked a large well lit up installation. Lieutenant Davis peered at the base though his binoculars.

"We found them, sir. This is where the future city and port of Veracruz would be. There is a large native city five kilometers inland having tens of thousands of inhabitants."

"Yes, lieutenant we did find them."

"Look at all those ships, sir. There must be at least ten warships docked in there, four of them steam frigates and the rest smaller sail powered warships." There was also a shipyard with a keel of a very large ship taking shape.

"It's dark and I can't really tell but it looks like they are laying down a very large ship in the yard."

"Let's camp here and we can check them out better in the morning. Make sure you post sentries, Leroy."

"Will do, sir."

"The team had awakened by sunrise had some dry rations for breakfast and prepared to depart the area for the long trip back."

"We got what we needed, sir. We need to get back and tell the general what we saw here. That is an ironclad they are building. I also spotted large coal dumps. It looks like they are using slaves. They need them to mine and transport the coal. It's very hard labor. I am sure the locals are not happy working for the Soviets."

"What's a ship of the line and why coal?"

"It's a very large armored ship with many heavy guns. Usually they had very heavy guns. They are also using coal to fire their boilers it burns hotter and longer."

"If they build a couple of those they can destroy our navies."

"They will be a generation ahead of us in ship design and

propulsion. We do have one up on them sir."

"Most of their ships will be crewed by be Aztecs. We have a naval tradition of a thousand years of sea fighting."

"We need to slow them down somehow, Said Davis as he scanned the base through his binoculars. "I see only one gun battery pointed out to sea and two pointed inland."

"What's that noise?"

"Everyone hit the ground and take cover now!"

The rest of the team ran into the woods and went to ground as the noise from the sky got louder. Everyone turned their gaze to the sky. Two aircraft on a biplane and the other a low wing monoplane flew overhead and headed up the coast. Lieutenant Davis was first to poke his head up. "Now we really have a problem they have aircraft. I saw guns on the biplane it looked like one the Soviets used in the second Great War. If they catch us on the water they will tear us to pieces."

"We will have to sail late in the evening till we put some distance between us and this base. We are lucky then had no flying machines patrolling."

"Thank god and Allah that we did not run into one."

"Let's get out of here and head home."

Interior of Vera Cruz, Mexico
August 13, 1454

After trudging through rough terrain for most of the day they had finally arrived early the next morning in a valley which had a large stream running through it. A small railroad ran east to west, possible to Mexico City and to the coast. Next to the stream was a large compound with wooden fortifications and guard towers encircling it. The team had camped on a small wooded hill that overlooked the valley. Logan looked through his binoculars and saw what looked to be European soldiers with AK47s manning the towers. Outside the fort was a small town that contained what looked to be a couple of smelters and another structure that had large tanks and many metal pipes around it. Around both facilities were stone bunkers with Russian soldiers in them guarding the approaches to the facilities.

A heavy smell of diesel oil permeated the area. Next to the smelter were several box cars with ore that was being unloaded by dozens of slaves guarded by Aztec soldiers carrying whips and muskets. "That's what they need slaves for lieutenant to do the dirty work for them."

They all heard a steam whistle and Longo spotted a train powered by a small steam engine pulling what looked to be tank cars coming from the east. The train finally stopped adjacent to the building with the tanks and pipes.

"It looks like the Soviets have created an industrial center, sir. What is that strange building with all the pipes? "

"I am not sure, Kemal. Several of our vehicles, including the fighting machine that came from the future need diesel oil for its engines. I remember General Mavrakis telling me that oil coming from the ground needs to be refined."

"So that's maybe a refinery?"

"It's very possible. I'll take a few pictures of it to show General Mavrakis."

"How will you take pictures, sir?"

"Watch and learn, lieutenant."

Longo took out a small cannon camera given to him by General Mavrakis that one of the Americans had brought with him from the future. The battery had been charged with a solar charger before they had left their base. Longo pointed the camera towards the city zoomed in and took several pictures. He then showed them to the Turkish officer who was amazed at the technology.

"In the name of Allah, that camera is amazing, sir."

"What's more amazing lieutenant is that it looks like the Russians have us beaten technology wise and we are in serious trouble."

"You are right. We need to get back and tell our commanders what is going on here, sir."

They all heard the sound of an engine coming from the east. They looked up and saw a bi-wing aircraft that was coming in for a landing. The plane landed adjacent to the fort, the gate was opened and the plane taxied inside the compound. Longo took several more pictures before the aircraft disappeared.

"Amazingly they also have flying machines. What else have they brought with them?"

"I don't want to get caught out here and find out, sir."

"We've seen enough lets go home."

Mexican coast, 150 miles North of Veracruz
August 19, 1454

After leaving Veracruz the commando team made their way back to their longboat and slowly headed up the cost traveling only during the late afternoon and camping on land during the night. The going was very slow trying to avoid detection from Soviet patrol ships that frequented that part of the coast. They had so far been successful in avoiding the patrols but all this was soon going to change. The longboat had been making good time with northerly breeze pushing them up the coast at 8 knots when suddenly they were becalmed a mile off the coast near a sandy strip of beach.

"Sail on the horizon, sir."

"We are screwed. There are no mangroves to hide in this time. If we reach the and beach the boat we will lose it and supplies. And the Russians will know we are here. Leroy, are you any good with that rocket device?"

Lieutenant Davis hesitated for a moment. "Sir, do you remember during the war the Ottoman powder supply convoy that blew up?"

"Yes I remember it very well. I lost many friends. Over a thousand men were killed and we lost many tons of valuable supplies."

"It was me that fired the rocket into one of the supply wagons carrying powder. I never expected such a huge explosion. I was picked up and thrown into the ground. I thought I was going to die."

For a moment Leroy though that Colonel Ali was going to attack him. He saw hatred in his eyes. He was almost ready to reach for his gun when the colonel took a deep breath. "It was war lieutenant. I would have done the same thing if I had the opportunity. You must be blessed by Allah if you survived such a tremendous explosion."

"Someone was definitly protecting me that day, sir."

"I hope that same luck holds out now, for all our sake."

"That ship can blow us out of the water. We will show no weapons until they are right up to us."

"What is the range of that thing?"

"We need to be no farther than 200 meters, if I am going to hit it"

"Maybe we can out run it with the outboard motor?"

"Then they will know we have futuristic equipment and they

may report it to their headquarters, sir. That will put all our friends at risk at the outpost if they sally with their fleet."

"You are right, Leroy. They may instead blow us out of the water if they think we are a risk."

"The wind," shouted one of the men.

"Raise the sails we can at least make like we are running away."

Soviet Steam Frigate Azov
August 19, 1454

Captain Yuri Petrovich peered through his field glasses at the small strange craft. They were still about four miles distant. This time he had also seen them. So far no one had heard anything more on the radio except for Russian. He would run the boat down and find out who they were.

"They've hoisted their sail, sir."

Yuri looked up at their sails and saw that the wind had returned albeit out of the south east. "How long before we have steam up, commander?"

"Another ten minutes, sir."

"Give me full speed as soon as we are able to. They should have had steam up 20 minutes ago, but his Aztec crew was almost useless. The Aztecs made good soldiers but terrible sailors."

"Yes, sir."

"I want them caught to find out what's going on. Neither the local natives nor Aztecs have these types of boats or rigs. They are may be European."

"How is that possible, sir?"

"I am hoping to find out commander."

"Could there be other time travelers?"

"Anything is possible. If the Soviet Union managed it then the Americans may have also mastered it."

"If they are Americans sir, we need to wipe them out. The Soviet empire must rule the world unopposed."

Ruling 15th century savages the captain thought to himself. "You are right commander, we must free the proletariat from the rule of despots," Captain Petrovich said telling his executive officer what he wanted to hear."

"Sir, engine room reports we have a full head of steam."

"Give me full speed now commander."

"Yes, sir."

Within a few minutes the Azov had reached her top speed of 11knots. "When we are close enough fire one of the guns across their bow to have them drop their sail."

"Yes, sir. We should be overhauling them in about 30-40 minutes sir."

"I am going to my cabin to a few minutes. Keep me informed if anything changes."

Coast of Veracruz.
August 19, 1454

With the wind blowing from the south west, the best speed longboat could make was five knots. The Soviet warship was slowly gaining on them. "Sir, they will have us in range with fifteen minutes."

"It seems that is our kismet (destiny) lieutenant. We will have to fight. There is no way we can outrun them."

"We could always make for the shore but we will lose the boat and be stranded without supplies."

"Then they will know if they haven't already figured it out that we are not from here."

"You are right sir we will have to fight. I will fire the RPG and Sergeants Kosmas and Ordun will shoot the grenade launchers, the rest will open up with the rifles and machine gun and may the lord protect us."

"If it is the will of Allah for us to survive we will do just that. Now everyone say a prayer and fire when the lieutenant shoots his RPG."

"There gaining on us," Sergeant Kosmas said. The Soviet frigate was now less than a mile away and closing on the long boat when its bow gun fired. The round shot landed 50 feet in front of the long boat.

"I need them closer, sir."

"We'll keep running some more."

Two minutes later the bow chaser gun fired again. The shot passed overhead and landed 25 feet away. "Drop the sail. They're less than 400 yards away. They'll be in range in less than minute."

"Attention you in the boat drop sails," someone shouted in English through a megaphone.

"Shit they made us," Davis said.

The sail was dropped and the small boat came to a stop. They could see the Soviet frigate coming closer. "Get ready guys. Give her all you got; spray the gun ports with the machine gun."

"May Allah protect us! Allah Akbar!"

"Let's do it!" Davis picked up the RPG 7 and fired. The RPG shell penetrated amidships and detonated in the engine room after hitting the boiler, setting off secondary explosions and blowing a large hole in the side of the ship. Flames and steam could be seen spewing out of it as it came to a complete stop. Both Sergeant Kosmas and Ordun fired their 40mm grenade launchers towards the frigate. One of the grenades exploded next to a barrel of gunpowder setting of another chain reaction of explosions. The rest of the team opened up with a machine gun and automatic weapons fire cutting down dozens of the surviving crew members.

"Wow we really hurt her bad."

Before Colonel Ali could reply a huge explosion rocked the frigate after the fire reached the powder room. "There she goes," Colonel Ali said.

The explosion had sent masts and spars into the air and broken the ship's back. They could hear hissing sound the hissing as the sea water put out the flames as the frigate quickly sank in 70 feet of water.

"Let's go see if there are any survivors, sir."

"Yes, we could use a prisoner to find out what's going on here."

The long boat reached the spot where the frigate had gone down. There were several bodies in the water many with horrible burns. "There," shouted Corporal Ahmet. Davis looked to where the soldier was pointing. There was a man holding on to a spar about 50 yards away.

"Let's go fish him out."

A minute later they were pulling him into the long boat. The man was blond, blue eyes with typical Slavic features vomited salt water over the side. "Get us out of here."

The sail was raised and the boat continued its journey up the coast. The man wearing an officer's uniform with four stripes on his epaulet said something in a language no one understood, except for Lieutenant Davis who knew it was Russian. "Do you speak English?"

"Yes, I would like some water."

"Davis handed him his canteen. The man took a long swig of water."

"You are an American the man said catching his breath?"

"Yes, my name is Lieutenant Leroy Davis Byzantine army."

"What? Byzantine army? The Byzantines were conquered by the Ottomans by this time"

"Who are you, Sir?"

The man by now had gotten his strength back. I am Captain Yuri Petrovich, commander of the former frigate Azov. You destroyed my ship and murdered my crew! All I remember was trying to climb on deck after the first explosion then hurtling through the air and waking up in the water"

"You fired on us, captain. I am sure once you found out who we were you would interrogate us and kill us."

The captain thought of what Leroy had just said. "I would not officially interrogate you, the GRU would. You do make a valid point."

By the way this is Lieutenant Colonel Ali Pasha, Ottoman Army and the mission commander."

"Hello captain," the Colonel said in heavy accented English. All Ottoman officers and NCOs had been mandated to learn English."

"You keep saying Byzantine and Ottoman army? How is this possible?"

Constantinopolis was never taken by the Ottoman in the siege. With our arrival and the weapons that came over with us we were able to help the Byzantines build a much stronger army and naval force to defeat the Ottomans completely. We actually saved the Sultan's life after his men tried assassinating him and helped him consolidate a new empire in central Asia Minor. To make a long story short we became friends and allies to survive in this new world."

"So the Americans have also developed time travel?"

"I wouldn't know that."

"So how did you travel to the 15th century?"

"Our convoy was attacked by the Taliban in Afghanistan and we fled with the few survivors into an old mine shaft we discovered. A suicide bomber blew himself up in the entrance trapping us inside. We traveled deeper and found an old Soviet underground base. We got the generator running but also activated some type of count down. When the countdown was over something strange happened to us. When we awakened and found a way out of the mine we found ourselves transported to eastern Thrace in the year 1452. We made contact with the Byzantines and allied with them. Now here we are."

"The Russian was shocked. "What year was it when you went into the Mine, Lieutenant Davis?"

"It was January 2014."

"My god! That's almost 26 years after we transited through. How is it you are in Afghanistan did you come to help the Soviet Union fight the Islamic extremists?'

"No captain. The Soviet Union no longer exists, it collapsed in 1991."

Captain Petrovich did not say a word. He was in total shock.

"Please tell me more."

Lieutenant Davis gave him a quick history lesson of what had occurred in the time period between the collapse of the Soviet Union and their arrival in 1452.

"So communism no longer exists in Russia?"

"No sir. It's a failed ideology. Moscow has become one of the most expensive cities in the world and has many billionaires living there. The government is autocratic and corrupt."

"Russians need strong men to rule them. Too bad about the corruption, that will never change in my country. So that is rather funny that the Mujahedeen attacked the people that created them."

"Unfortunately, that is what extreme fundamentalist Islam created, Al-Qaida and ISIS. Hopefully we can prevent that scourge from ever happening."

"So our outpost here in the new world is the only chance of making a true Soviet empire."

"If you want to call being stuck in the middle of the 15th century, a great time to build a Soviet Empire."

"You do have a point ieutenant. Unfortunately that will not dissuade General Balkov the commander of this operation. He is determined to rule the world."

"Well he has a long way to go," added Colonel Ali. "My English is not best but I understood much of what you said.

"That is true but with our technical knowledge the supplies we brought and the thousands of slaves at our disposal he may succeed."

"What do you mean technical knowledge?"

"We were not all soldiers that came over, Lieutenant. Many were scientists, engineers, miners, technicians and craftsmen."

"That may be true captain but we have one thing over you and that is freemen. They don't have to fear the whip or death. They do it for the good of their families and country."

"Fear and pain also work well, lieutenant."

"Yes they do. That is another reason the Soviet Union collapsed. Its satellite states wanted freedom."

"That is all in the future. So tell me where are you taking me?"

"To rendezvous with our warship then to our base up north and eventually, Constantinopolis."

"I would love to see the seat of Orthodoxy and a civilized city. Don't know how civilized it will be in the 15th century though?"

"You will be very surprised when you see the city. Many changes have occurred since we arrived. You will even meet Emperor Constantine XI."

"The warrior emperor! It would be such an honor. I am actually tired of this place and General Balkov and his methods. I am looking to a new start."

"He is a good man and a wise ruler. Be prepared for many surprises."

CHAPTER 11

Coast of Veracruz
August 20, 1454

After walking for several days Colonel Longo and his team finally reached the Atlantic coast. The trip back had been more difficult having to avoid Aztec patrols and scout aircraft. Longo was sure that by now the Soviets had missed the patrol they had killed and had search parties out to look for them. When they reached the waterfront they had found the Limnos waiting anchored in the bay. Longo signaled the ship and a long boat was sent out to pick them up. Dirty, tired and hungry they were all glad to have made it back in once piece. General Mavrakis, Colonel Ali and Commander Green were waiting for them when they climbed up the rope ladder to the deck.

"Welcome back, colonel."

"Glad to be back."

"How did it go?"

"We found the Russians. The must have been here for a while. We found one of their manufacturing centers and base. They had a railroad that brought oil to a refinery and ore to an iron factory. They also have the Aztecs as their allies."

"Yes we found the Soviets too. They've been here about five years," Colonel Ali said.

Longo heard the Anchor going up and the paddle wheels started to turn. "We are leaving already?"

"Yes, we don't want to run into the Soviet navy."

"How do you know they were here for five years, Ali?"

Colonel Ali ran into a large steam frigate a generation ahead of what we got. It had a screw propeller instead of paddle wheels. Fortunately he was able to sink it with the use of RPGs. He picked up a survivor, Yuri Petrovich the ship's captain. He told us everything about the Russians. He actually volunteered the information."

"We are in serious danger if the Soviets make a move now. We are not ready for them, sir.

"I know that, they're building an ironclad in their shipyard. If they come across the Atlantic with that, we may not be able to stop them. We need to slow them down."

"What's an ironclad?"

"It's an armored warship," Commander Green answered.

"We don't have the ability to stop that."

"No we don't, Colonel Longo. At least not yet. We will need heavier guns"

"Commander, I want everyone in my cabin in 30 minutes. In the meantime change course and head and due east until out of sight of land then turn south."

"Aye, aye, general."

Twenty Miles off the Coast of Vera Cruz
August 20, 1454

George looked around the table at those present. The seriousness of what had to be done showed in everyone's face. They would soon need to make a decision that could cost them all their lives. "Gentlemen, to all those that have not met our new guest, I would like to introduce you to Captain Yuri Petrovich, commander of the former Soviet Frigate Azov. He has decided to join our cause."

"I am honored to meet you all. I want to thank General Mavrakis for accepting me to join your cause. Some of you may not trust me but hopefully my actions will prove you wrong. I will tell you that the Soviets have laid down the roots to build a mighty empire. That is our mission here and General Vladimir Balkov the Soviet commander is a ruthless man that will stop at nothing to accomplish the the task.

The options we have are few. The Soviets are years ahead of us. They are building an infrastructure that will pour out weapons in a massive scale. They have tens of thousands of Aztec allies that will fight for them. Within a year or two they will cross the Atlantic and begin their conquest of Europe. No one will be able to stop them."

"Then we need to hit them were it will hurt them the most. We need to attack their naval base and take out as many of their ships that we can, sir."

"How do we do that Colonel Ali and not get blown out of the water?"

"They only have two shore batteries guarding the approaches from the sea. Most of their guns are pointing towards land, sir. We land a force and take out those guns. The have some radar but they never run it. They won't be suspecting an attack from the sea in 1454. The Europrans haven't discovered this continent yet."

"That's true. The Azov has only been missing for two days. Their patrols can last from a week to ten days according to Captain Petrovich. We've also not been using our radio. So hopefully they will have dropped their guard."

"What about the radio? Their headquarters won't be receiving any radio checks?"

"Radios do break down, commander, "Captain Petrovich said. "It's common for patrols to fail to check in."

"So we attack tomorrow night an hour before daybreak. Colonel Longo you and your team will take out the coastal batteries at the entrance then attack any targets of opportunity, hopefully they can get to the iron clad being built in the shipyard and damage or destroy it. You will take along several LAWS and the 50mm mortar to help you accomplish your mission. You will take Lieutenant Davis with you. He knows where the gun batteries are situated and knows how to use the mortar. Once the guns are neutralized, we will head for the harbor."

"We will get it done, sir."

"I know you will."

"Colonel Ali you and your team will paddle into the harbor under cover of darkness and attempt to cut out the remaining screw powered steam frigate from her anchorage once the coastal batteries are neutralized. You will take also several sailors along to help you sail the ship. According to Captain Petrovich, she is the 2800 ton Sebastopol. She is armed with 24 VIII Dalgreen guns. All shoot 50 pound shells and 65 lb solid shot. Most of her 200 man crew will be ashore. There should only be about 20 men aboard, most of them asleep. If we pull it off, we will sail her home and copy the technology. That would also neutralize much of the Soviet Navy. They still will have four heavily steam paddle frigates armed with 32 pounder guns and several corvettes and sloops.

"Wow with those armaments the Sebastopol alone could sink much of our navy before we over powered her by sheer numbers."

"That is probably a true statement, Commander Green. Those

Dahlgreen guns were the pinacle of naval smoth bore canon. The Limnos will enter the anchorage and attack the ships at anchor. If we can completely surprise them, it should allow us to raise some havoc. Colonel Ali in the interval you and your men will prepare a tow line so we can pull the Sebastopol out of the anchorage."

"We'll be ready, sir."

"Now get some rest and in the morning prepare your teams."

Vera Cruz, Mexico
August 22, 1454

The Limnos had been waiting off shore out of sight of land till just after midnight. Once George had given the order the ship turned towards the west and sailed towards the shore at a leisurely six knot. Once she had reached the landing zone she dropped off the two commando teams. Colonel Longo and his team under the cover of darkness had reached the shore about a mile up the coast from the gun batteries. The heavily armed team slowly worked their way south towards the guns following the tree line. Davis motioned for everyone to halt.

"I see six men sir. We can't get any closer without being seen. The first gun battery is straight ahead about 150 meters from here."

"Okay, let's do it men."

The four men that were chosen to take out the second gun battery put their weapons and packs down and headed for the water's edge armed only with knives and cross bows. Leroy and Colonel Longo crawled closer towards the closest guns with their suppressed M4 rifles. "Were close enough, sir. Stand by to fire. I see our guys they should be firing their cross bows any second."

"I am ready. I see them to."

"Fire!"

"Both men opened fire quickly taking out the targets."

The four men in the water fired their crossbows taking out four of the gunners. Two of the Ottoman commandos came out scimitars drawn and quickly cut down the Aztec soldiers before they could raise their muskets.

The rest of the team quickly ran to the guns and began spiking the touch holes making them unable to fire. Longo took out his flash light and began signaling the Limnos. Within a few seconds the signal was returned. "There on their way, Davis. Let's go do some damage."

While Longo's team was spiking the guns at the harbor's entrance, Colonel's Ali's team had silently paddled their Zodiac to the Sebastopol which was anchored in the middle of the bay next to one of the paddle steamer frigates.

"We haven't been discovered yet, sir. We've been lucky so far, let's hope it holds." The zodiac reached the side of the ship and was secured while two grapnel hooks were thrown up over the ships railings. Two men quickly climbed to the deck and reappeared a minute later.

"The guards been neutralized come on up." The rest of the twelve man team climbed aboard. Ali looked at the watch George had lent him, it was 0545hrs.

Yiannis, Mehmet go to the front and prepare a towline. If we have to we cut the anchor cable we'll do it. Lieutenant Aturk the rest of the men and secure the rest of the ship's crew. No shooting crossbows and swords only."

"Yes, sir."

A few minutes later Lieutenant Aturk and his men appeared with 40 prisoners. "Is this all of them lieutenant?"

"We had to neutralize a few of them who would not come quietly."

"Did you find any Russians?"

"No, sir."

"Watch out!" Before the two men could react a gun shot rang out dropping one of the Aztec sailors that was holding a small blade.

"Sorry, sir I had to shoot him."

"Thanks Pavlos, for saving my ass."

"You owe me one, Lieutenant."

"I'm sure everyone heard the gunshot."

"Suddenly a flare let the sky over the anchorage.

Ali could see the Limnos entering the harbor. Her guns opened fire on several smaller ships that were anchored near the entrance. The heavy rounds were tearing them to match sticks. "Lieutenant, cut the anchor and throw the crew overboard, give them a long boat and anything that can float."

"Yes, sir."

Ali heard the familiar thump of a light mortar firing, followed by an explosion inside the naval base. "That must be Longo. Make ready to get under way."

Soviet Naval Base, Vera Cruz, Mexico
August 22, 1454

Admiral Georgi Timoshenko was awakened by the sound of gunfire. He looked out the window of the headquarters building and saw several ships and building ablaze in the harbor. The base was under attack but that should be impossible during this time period. No one should have the military capability in 1454 to cause such destruction. Another flare reached skywards illuminating the unknown ship as it fired another broadside at one of his paddle wheel frigates. He was shocked with what he saw as the flare illuminated a large paddle wheel steam frigate firing heavy guns at various targets in the bay. He also heard the sound of automatic weapons fire.

"This is impossible!" He said out loud. Grabbing his cloths he started to get dressed and headed outside to take command of a disaster in the making. General Balkov would also need to be appraised and he dreaded what Balkov would do.

Using the attack of the Limnos as his deversion, Colonel Longo headed for the ship yards, but the going was becoming tougher as the base was beginning to awaken and officers were starting to rally their troops. "Sir I don't think we can get much closer without getting trapped here."

"I think you are right, Lieutenant. We can't hang around here too long. Can you hit the ship with the RPGs and mortars?"

"It's about 300 meters but I think I can hit it," said Davis as he took the RPG from his shoulder and aimed it toward the ironclad ship being built in the ship yard. The rocket flew true and struck the ship amidships causing a small explosion and starting a fire. Davis set up the mortar and began lobbing 50mm shells towards the ship. Several of the mortar bombs landed on or around the Ironclad and started several fires.

"Those last four rounds landed on target," we have done her enough damage Davis let's get out of here."

"You have another RPG why don't you use it?"

"We may need it for out escape."

"Yes, that may be needed. Let's go."

"I'm with you, sir. Let's get the hell out of here," Davis said as he lobed several shells on the advancing troops.

"Men, we're heading back to the beach," Yelled Longo, as

they began a fighting withdrawal back towards the rubber raft.

Colonel Ali watched as the Limnos pounded the adjacent frigate while her crew jumped overboard to escape the devastating cannon fire. In the interval the Sebastopol had floated away from it anchorage with the outgoing tide. Ali's men had used the crew to raise the anchor before tossing them overboard. The few sailors that Ali had brought along had been made a towline using the remainder of the anchor cable.

The sun had begun to rise and the darkness had given way to burning ships and buildings. The Byzantine frigate drew in front of the Sebastopol and stopped. Several sailors began yelling to bring the tow line over. Two men climbed down to the rubber raft and paddled to the front of the ship grabbed the heavy hemp tow line and transported it across the short distance to the Limnos. Several sailors belonging to the engine room crew jumped into the zodiac and rowed to the captured frigate and climbed aboard after securing the Zodiac to the ship. Commander Green gave the order to the ships engine room for all ahead slow. The paddle wheels began to turn and quickly took up the slack. The ship shuddered as the weight of the Soviet frigate fought the tow line. For a while it looked like nothing was going to happen but soon ever so slowly the large screw frigate began to move. A loud cheer could be heard coming from both ships. With the tide outgoing the Limnos with the capuured soviet arship in tow headed towards the mouth of the harbor about a half a mile way at three knots.

"Engine room can you give me a couple of more revolutions?"

"We are straining the engine, sir. She was not made to tow 3000 tons. I'll see what I can do," the chief engineer said.

Admiral Timoshenko had made contact with his command

staff and they had begun to bring some semblance of order. "Sir they cut out the Sebastopol."

Timoshenko peered through his binoculars at the lead paddle wheel steamer pulling the Sebastopol towards the harbor entrance. He looked at the yellow flag flying above it with two eagles it somewhat looked familiar. He had seen it before. "Sir the BMP is here."

"Commander Popov, have them stop that ship from escaping, now!"

"Yes, sir!"

After bypassing or fighting their way through the base they had finally reached the Zodiac, the started the engine and headed for the harbors entrance to meet the ships.

"There is the Limnos, sir. Oh shit! There is an AFV at the entrance. It's a BMP1 and it's got a canon on it that can blow the frigate out of the water. They haven't noticed us yet. Take us in I need to take it out with the RPG before it sinks the frigate."

The Limnos was just nearing the harbor entrance when a cannon shell from the BMP struck her bow and exploded in her anchor locker killing one crew man. Several of the frigate's guns returned fire striking the AVF with a 32 lb. round shot just as the gunner was about to fire denting the armor and shaking up the crew inside but causing no real damage. The cannon shell went wide missing the frigate. By this time Davis had reached the shoreline and ran towards the vehicle. Fortunately for him the crew of the BMP was fixated on the two ships trying to leave the harbor and did not notice him till it was too late. Davis raised the rocket tube and fired just as the BMP fired a third round and the vehicle's machine gunner opened up. At 150 meters it was almost impossible to miss a stationary target. The 93mm HEAT round designed to destroy heavy MB tanks easily penetrated the 33mm thick armor and exploded blowing the turret out like a corkscrew. There were no survivors. The 73mm cannon shell struck the Byzantine frigate amidships and exploded in the crew quarters killing and injuring several sailors and starting a fire.

Longo and the rest of the team watched the destruction of the BMP1 and Lieutenant Leroy Davis go down. Longo and two other men ran towards the fallen American. When they reached him they saw blood pouring out of a leg wound. "Leroy, are you okay?"

"I've been shot and it hurts as hell." They applied a dressing and carried their wounded comrade back to the Zodiac and started the outboard and headed for the Limnos which had at this point had left the harbor and was headed out towards open water trailing thick smoke.

Admiral Timoshenko watched in horror through his binoculars the short, but deadly battle at the harbors entrance. He saw the BMP fire on the frigate and then blow up as it was struck by an anti-tank rocket just as the two ships exited the harbor. The enemy frigate had been damaged, but not fatally. There was not much he could do now his command had been wrecked. Most of the fleet had been sunk at anchor or severely damaged. To make matters even worse, they lost one of their precious fighting vehicles. There would be hell to pay when General Balkov found out the extent of the disaster.

"They got away, sir."

"I can see that, Major."

"Sir, the Ironclad was severely damaged. It was hit by an RPG and several mortar rounds. The fire was finally put out."

"My god! Who could these people be? Where they

Americans? Did they also perfect time travel?"

"I don't know sir," replied the marine officer, "but I found these."

"Let me see, major."

"These are 7.62x39 caliber brass casings used by an AK47. Are you sure they came from their weapons?"

"Yes, sir. Our troops were using muskets."

"So they were using Soviet Weapons?

"Yes sir, they were."

"They too must be from the future. Now I remember that flag of theirs. I remember it as a little boy when my mother dragged me to church. That yellow flag with the two eagles was the flag of Byzantium!"

"Byzantium, sir? Constantinopolis should have fallen last year after a short siege to the Turks."

"That is correct, major but something must have drastically changed the time line. That was a Byzantine flag on a steam powered war ship. We are not the only ones here from the future. The game has changed."

That evening, just before sunset, General Vladimir Balkov commander of all Soviet forces in the new world, was flown in by one of the three MI-4 helicopters that had been brought with them to the 15th century. He was met upon arrival by a worried Admiral Timoshenko.

"I hope your flight went well, sir."

The general looked around at the still smoldering building and sunken and damaged ships at their anchorages. "What the hell happened here, Timoshenko?"

"We were attacked from the sea, sir."

"I can see that you idiot."

"Who did this?

"I am not certain, sir. They came with a paddle wheel steam ship, mounting large naval cannon. They landed troops that were armed with AK47s and crossbows. They took out the BMP with an RPG."

"What? That is not possible in this era. Steam ships are at least 400 years in the future and proper naval guns won't make their appearance for another 150 years. Could it be the Americans or Chinese?"

"I don't know, sir. The enemy warship was flying a yellow flag with a double headed eagle with a crown above its head and a Greek symbol that looked the letter PI."

"Are you out of your mind, admiral? That is the Byzantine flag under the Paleologos dynasty. I am well versed in Byzantine history."

"I know it sounds insane, sir. But many of my officers and men saw the same flag flying on the mast of that ship. We did not imagine it."

"How would that be possible? Byzantium was only a shell of itself by the 15th century and should have fallen to the Turks last year!"

"Unless the Americans or someone else has travelled back in time and helped the Byzantines modernize and defeat the Ottomans. There is no other way to explain it, general."

"Yes, yes there is no other way to explain it. The strange language that some heard on the radio had to be Greek. Not men from mars that some fools thought. We must immediately find and sink that ship."

"Sir, I have more bad news. The Azov has not reported in. We must consider her lost."

"What do we have left?"

"Nothing, sir, except for a few lightly armed sloops we lost all our major surface units. We can't take on that warship and the Sebastopol together. We don't even know if they have other ships with them. They could have built a base anywhere on the continent."

"What of the iron clad?"

"It's been seriously damaged, sir. It will take many months to repair the damage if even possible."

"This is a disaster! I am just as responsible for this. None of us ever dreamed we would have any enemies capable of crossing the Atlantic and fighting us. We must now prepare ourselves for a much longer struggle. In a way this disaster could be a blessing in disguise Imagine had we sailed to Europe and encountered a large enemy fleet just as technologically advanced. We could have been totally destroyed. Now we know better."

"Yes, sir. We will rebuild and destroy our enemies."

"I want search planes sent out to look for the enemy ships."

"Yes, sir. I will order scouts out at daybreak."

Gulf of Mexico, 130 miles NE Vera Cruz Mexico 24 August 1454

Once they had cleared the harbor entrance both ships raised their sails and headed out to sea on a southeast course to throw off any pursuers. When they had finally sailed out of sight of land the two ships stopped to make repairs and exchange crew. Thanks to superb training by Commander Green, the damage control parties were able to quickly put the fires out and begin repairs on the Limnos. By this time they had started the boilers on the Soviet Frigate, Green's engineers were able to figure out the working of the engine and get the ship underway.

Daybreak had found the two warships under full sail heading north towards their outpost on the future Texas-Mexico border. George wanted to reach their base as soon as possible and evacuate back across the Gulf of Mexico towards Florida. They had awakened a hornet's nest and he was sure the Russians would be looking for them. He would not be proven wrong.

George had been sipping his coffee on the bridge of the Limnos when Commander Green walked in. "Sir, I have posted lookouts and have manned the machine guns as you asked.

"Thanks, commander. I am not worried about the Soviet navy we've destroyed most of their ships that would be a threat to us. We are still within range of their aircraft and if I was that Soviet commander I would have my aircraft looking for those ships."

"I hope they don't find us, sir. We really don't have any anti-air weapons other than the machine guns and AK47."

"Commander Green, I want everyone armed. We probably have a couple of hours till they find us. If we put out enough lead we may get lucky. Keep us heading west. We will hopefully be out of range by this evening."

"Aye, aye, sir."

When all the marines and soldiers had been called out and armed, George gave them instructions on shooting down aircraft by leading it and firing short bursts. Those having single fire Muskets and Nagants would fire on command. Hopefully with concentrated fire they could put a few rounds into a plane and scare it away. He also sent ten marines and a machinegun over to the Sebastopol, so it too could have some anti-air coverage and ordered the boilers lit on both ships and then sails lowered to prevent any fires if they were attacked.

Just a few minutes after the two ships had switched to steam power, the lookouts spotted an aircraft flying in from the southwest. "Go to general quarters," George commanded. Colonel Longo ran to the DSHK machine gun that had been mounted on the bow and the marines lined up in the back to concentrate there rifle and machine gun fire. George peered through his binoculars and spotted the aircraft. He was surprised to see that it was a biplane. He remembered from the many WW2 documentaries that he had seen that the Soviets had used an obsolete biplane to harass the Nazis at night. It was called a PO2. He knew the plane could carry a decent bomb load and a light machine gun. If they had bombs no matter their size they were screwed.

Major Gyorgy Rodenko and his observer and friend Sergeant Sergei Pavlov, had taken off a little after daybreak flying due west at an altitude of 2000 meters. The PO2 designed and first flown in the late 1920s was a dependable aircraft and easy to maintain. Even though it was probably older than him, he had utmost confidence in the old biplane, since he did most of the maintenance on the plane by himself. His degree was in aeronautical engineering which he had received upon graduation from the Soviet Union's Yuri Gagarin Air force academy. He had been a test pilot at the Mikoyan factory for the Mig-31 prototype, when the call for volunteer pilots for a special project, flying obsolete biplanes had been posted. Gyorgy had been one of the first to volunteer.

He had been flying on the same heading at a cruising speed of 60 knots for the last couple of hours. Pretty soon he would have to turn around and return, if he wanted to make it back before running out of fuel. That was one of the disadvantages of the PO2 it only had a cruising range of 400 miles. If they had to ditch this far out at sea, there was no way they would be rescued. Sea traffic in this part of the world was non-existent in this century. Unfortunately for him fate had other ideas for him. Just as he was about to turn around he noticed a black smudge on the horizon it was definitely smoke. He had found the enemy ships. He quickly reported their position and was given orders to attack the enemy ship. Gyorgy pointed at the ship and had Pavlov arm his machine gun.

"Sir, I see the paddle wheel steamer flying the flag of Byzantium. That is crazy. They should not be here and even crazier they are in a stream powered warship."

He pushed the stick forward putting the plane into a shallow dive towards the enemy ship. He would fly alongside it and have Pavlov strafe the ship from bow to stern.

"Here he comes. Everyone on the starboard side and prepare to fire on my command. We have one shot let's make it count. Don't forget to lead the plane. After you have fired your muskets hit the deck and take cover."

George picked up his M4 flicked the selector to auto and watched the plane coming closer. When the plane reached the bow he gave the order to fire. Over 100 muskets AK-47s and the DSHK heavy machine gun opened fire at the slow moving plane. At the same moment a Sergeant Pavlov opened fire with the mounted ShKAS 7.62mm machine gun. Gyorgy felt the plane shudder as it was struck by several bullets. He felt a sharp pain as a 58 caliber Mini ball punched through his thigh fortunately missing the bone. His gunner was not as lucky. Gyorgy looked back and saw Sergeant Pavlov slumped over in his seat. A 7.62 round had gone through his stomach and out his back.

"Sergei, are you hit bad?"

"I am gut shot, sir. The bullet went out my back. I am bleeding pretty badly."

The engine was starting to sputter from lack off fuel. A bullet had punctured a fuel line. With his rear gunner seriously wounded and with his engine begging to fail, Gyorgy decided to ditch the plane near one of the ships. He would rather be a prisoner then fish food. Besides, Pavlov would probably bleed out pretty soon if he did not get medical attention.

After the plane had passed George gave the order to cease fire. They had come out of the engagement fairly unscathed. Several machine gun rounds had struck the ship lightly wounding two men. Everyone could hear the plane's engine begin to sputter. The pilot turned the plane towards the ships and was waved a white scarf. "Everybody hold your fire. He is going to try and put the plane down. "Commander, lunch a boat to pick them up. I am going over with it. I want us close to the plane, maybe we can hoist it aboard before it sinks."

"Will do, sir."

Everyone silently watched as the pilot pulled the plane's nose up to slow it down as it got lower; finally stalling out it hit the sea. The plane's landing gear dug into the water causing the plane to nose into the sea. For a moment everyone thought it would flip over but it finally righted itself. The pilot quickly got out and went to help his wounded observer get out before the plane sank. The Limnos' crew had lowered one of the Zodiacs in record time, which quickly made it over to the ditched plane. George threw a rope towards. "Hold on to the rope," he yelled out in English.

Two sailors jumped into the water and helped the pilot and the injured observer to the Zodiac. George noticed that both men were bleeding. He reached for the first aid kit. The pilot noticed George's rank and name tag along with the Beretta pistol he had in his holster. "General Americanski military?"

"Da, yes, I am American but in the Byzantine military."

"Very interesting, the Byzantine military. Now please help my friend. He is wounded very badly," the pilot said in heavily accented English.

"We will help you and your friend the best we can."

By now the Limnos had pulled next to the plane. Several sailors had jumped into the sea and tied ropes around the half sunken plane to keep it from going under.

George looked up and saw Commander Green looking over the railing. "Green, I have seriously wounded men here. Tell the doctor to prepare for casualties. Need some help to hoist them aboard?"

Ten minutes later the two wounded airmen had been hoisted aboard and taken to sickbay. In the interval they had saved the plane from sinking and had hoisted it partially out of the water. "We can't bring it aboard as is, sir. If we bring the plane any closer the wings will smash against the ship.

"Then we take her apart the best we can, commander."

By late evening the plane had been disassembled as best as the Byzantine engineers and mechanics could and hoisted the parts aboard. Most of the larger parts including the fuselage with the motor had been secured in the stern section. The plane had been washed with fresh water and the engine given a light coat of grease before being covered with canvas and tightly lashed to the deck. By nightfall both ships were heading north at full speed.

Chapter 12

Gulf of Mexico, 200 Miles South of Texas Border
August 25, 1454

The next morning George visited the ships' sickbay to check on the two wounded Russians. The observer had been seriously wounded and had to undergo emergency surgery. "Good morning doctor Makriyannis. How are your two patients doing?"

"Major Rodenko will be fine. His wound was not life threatening. His friend though, Sergeant Pavlov was seriously injured and lost a lot of blood. The bullet passed through his stomach but did not hit any vital organs. I did all I could but he is still in serious condition. He can also thank Commander Green if he makes it for giving him a liter and a half of blood."

"What's his prognosis, doctor?"

"He is very strong. If no infection sets in, he may make it." If anyone could save him George though, it would be doctor Makriyannis. He had been his wife's best student.

George looked up as another man walked into sick bey. "Good morning, General."

"Good morning Captain Petrovich. Come to check on your friends?"

"Yes, I do know the pilot. He is a good man. If I talk to him he may even join us."

"That would be very good for all, if you could accomplish that."

"I will do my best. I think he will come around. Maybe both of them will, if the observer survives his wounds."

The two men walked over to the cot where Major Rodenko was laying in. Rodenko was awake having just finished breakfast and totally surprised when he saw Captain Petrovich walk in. "Yuri, what are you doing here? He asked in Russian."

"Excuse me for a minute, General Mavrakis. I will speak to my friend here in Russian it will be much easier to explain to him the present situation he is in."

"Yes go right ahead, captain."

"Same thing as you my friend, Yuri replied in Russian."

"What happened to your ship?"

"It was sunk with all hands. I was lucky enough to be blown into the sea and rescued."

"How was this possible? She was heavier armed then this ship?"

"We tried to stop a small long boat containing several elite troops and they hit us with RPGS and blew us out of the water. Who would suspect that they would be armed with RPGs, in 1454?"

"That is true, Yuri. Who are these people? Are they really who they say?"

"Yes, my friend they are units of the Byzantine military force."

"But how is this possible? The Americans have developed time travel?"

"No, they were fighting Jihadists in Afghanistan almost 25 years after we withdrew. They were ambushed and the survivors fled to an underground mine. The same one we were transported back in time from. Somehow they activated the sequence and were transported to Eastern Thrace, to the year 1452."

"But how is that possible? We were transported from there. We brought everything with us, the entire base!"

"I have no idea my friend. No one really knows how time travel works. Maybe a hole is opened to another dimension. Maybe they were getting ready to send another mission through and something happened. You remember those demons that were flying above us when we were transporting here?"

"Yes, how can I forget?"

"These Americans that came through the portal made contact with the Byzantines and with the equipment they found inside the base and with their knowledge helped them modernize their military and navy and defeated the Ottomans. Now they are a major world power and have allied themselves with the Ottomans whom they displaced to central Anatolia."

"Wow, the world is really changing."

"Yes, maybe for the better. The Byzantines are trying to build a world of free men where hard work pays dividends and all men are equal in god's eyes. They asked me if I would like to join them and I agreed. I am sick and tired of Balkov and his cruelties. Will you join us Gyorgy?"

"The pilot looked towards his observer who was still hooked to a primitive IV. "The doctor tells me he has a good chance to make it."

"I hope so, we've been friends for so many years, I was going to put him in to promotion for lieutenant but Balkov said Sergei lacked the revolutionary zeal to be an officer. Yes, I will join you to make a better world and defeat Balkov."

"Thank you, Major."

Petrovich turned to George and changed to English. "General the major would like to join your cause."

George held out his hand and the wounded pilot took it.

"Welcome to the Byzantine air force, major." The major gave him a funny stare, "air force?"

"Yes, we also have aircraft. Your friend will be given a commission as a captain if he servives."

"Thank you, sir."

Byzantine Base, Texas Border
August 27, 1454

After another day and a half of sailing they finally reached their outpost on the future Texas-Mexico border. Almost immediately General Mavrakis called a war council to brief everyone on the raid on the Soviet Base. They would quickly need to make future plans. Every senior officer was present including the two Russian officers. The mood around the table was festive, everyone was ecstatic on their recent victory and capture of the Soviet steam frigate. But the elation would not last for long. "We should go and capture their base and destroy them before they recover, General Mavrakis."

"According to our new Russian friends, General Balkov is a very capable and ruthless commander. He would have by now deployed his aircraft to the adjacent airstrip. The PO2 aircraft we salvaged can carry a bomb load of 250 kilos for 200 miles. They have at least two more and several other smaller planes and helicopters. They would blow us out of the water before we even got close to the base. Additionally he would have used his rail road to transport Aztec reinforcements to the coast."

'I am sure they soon will be looking for us."

"Yes, general, they will," replied Captain Petrovich. General Balkov will take your attack personally and not rest until he finds and destroys you. He will bring hundreds of slaves to repair the damage and raise the ships that were sunk. He will build many more ships and come at you with them and a huge army."

"Then we need to go back home and build our armies and prepare."

"He also has in his possession a super weapon that can destroy an entire city."

"A nuclear bomb? Asked Colonel Longo.

"You know about this weapon?"

"I heard of these weapons and how you almost destroyed the world with them?"

"Well, we brought one with us."

"In the name of Allah how do we stop them now?"

"There may be one in the tunnels in the underground base. We are still making discoveries."

"Let's pray there is one there my friend. Or as you say we are screwed."

"We will leave in three days. We are in the middle of hurricane season and the going back may be very rough. We will need to have a full complement of fuel to ride out any storm. Captain Petrovich you will take command of our latest acquisition. She will be named the St Petersburg in honor of St Peter.

"I will be honored, sir."

Five days later while on the bridge the duty officer came in looking for George.

"Sir, there is a General Vladimir Balkov on the radio, asking in English for the Byzantine commander."

"Thank you. I think I will have a chat with him. Please have General Ismail Bay and Colonel Longo, meet me in the radio room immediately."

"Yes, sir."

George proceeded to the radio room while the duty officer went to find the two officers. When George walked into the radio room heard a voice speaking in accented English.

"This is General Balkov, Soviet commander in the Americas. I wish to speak to the Byzantine military commander."

George picked up the mike. "This is Lieutenant General George Mavrakis task force commander."

"So I can tell from your accent, you are an American. That means the Americans have also mastered time travel?"

"Well we are here," replied George, not wanting to tell the Russian the truth.

"How dare you attack the Soviet Union?"

"The Soviet Union and the Warsaw pact disintegrated without a shot being fired in 1989, General. It was replaced by the Russian federation."

"You are lying."

"No general. We are from the year 2015. The Russian Federation is ruled today by a democratically elected, but authoritarian president named Vladimir Putin. Most of the Soviet republics and former Warsaw pact states are now independent countries. Some even joined NATO. The Russian military is only a fraction of what it once was."

"I knew a KGB Colonel named Putin. I met him before we came here."

"That is the same person."

"Then mother Russia is in good hands. He would never surrender to the Americans!"

"He is starting to become a pain in the Ukraine, trying to regain Russian influence."

"That is our sphere of influence general."

"You also lost in Afghanistan and signed a peace accord in Dec 1989. This war also hastened the collapse of the Soviet Union. George knew he hit a sore spot because of the loss of the underground base. Balkov knew he was now trapped in time."

"So tell me what the world is like?"

"China is now very rich and becoming a super power. The western world is at war with radical Islamists."

"Thank for the United states for arming and emboldening them in Afghanistan."

"We fought a war in Iraq and got rid of Saddam Hussein and now Islamists are fighting all over the middle east, We are are also in Afghanistan fighting the Jihadists after they crashed two planes into the twin towers in NY, knocking them down killing 3000 people. Russia is also fighting Islamists in Chechnya."

"You reap what you sow, general. You will reap hell when we meet and be assured that will happen. I will chase you to the ends of the earth. I will create a socialist empire that will rule the world."

"Not if I have anything to do with it."

"So tell me General Mavrakis. How is a Greek American General fighting for the Byzantines? There should no longer be a Byzantine empire. It should now be the Ottoman Empire. Mehmet the conqueror should have taken the city last year."

"Upon our arrival we helped the Byzantines modernize and build weapons and cannon. With those and our help they managed to defeat the Ottoman siege and destroy the Ottoman army. We helped the Sultan when his troops mutinied and seriously wounded him. We saved his life and helped him establish a new empire in Asia Minor. We are now friends and allies with the Ottomans."

"My, my, how history has been radically changed."

"The world will be positively changed for the better."

"It will be changed general, especially when it's united under one Soviet Empire!"

"That won't happen, General Balkov. Oh and by the way, don't count on the Azov. We sank her too."

"Just one more reason for us to succeed, General Mavrakis. We will destroy you, count on it. Putin knows we are here and he will find a way to contact us. Goodbye, for now General Mavrakis."

With that Balkov closed the contact. No one said a word. George knew they had a mortal enemy who would one day be at their gates. "Gentlemen we now have a very serious problem."

Sultan's Palace, Konya
28 August 1454

The Security Council meeting had been called after receiving the last radio message from General Mavrakis. The emperor had flown to Konya to consult with the sultan for a new rearmaments plan after the battle of Veracruz. In the absence of General Mavrakis the emperor had nominated Major Jenkins to serve as his security advisor. The young sultan had brought his wife to the meeting who also served as his security advisor and commander of the military academy with the rank brigadier general. Most of the Byzantine and Ottoman general staff were also present. Constantine as the senior partner of the alliance was first to speak. "Ladies and gentlemen, we called this meeting because we now have a serious crisis on our hands. We all know of the successful battle of Vera Cruz. General Mavrakis and his forces managed to destroy most of the Soviet fleet including the ironclad they were building and severely damaged the base. We have now learned that the Soviet commander a General Balkov has communicated with General Mavrakis and told him that he intends to create a global Soviet Empire. He also promised to destroy us in the process. We can't allow that to happen. We have at least a year to prepare. The Soviets will have to rebuild their navy and amass an army. Our expedition is on the way back. General Mavrakis is returning with the captured Russian warship which is propelled with a screw, (propeller). That is the next generation in propulsion and with Major Jenkins help and out new Russian friends we will be able to reverse engineer and build an ironclad. We will have to pool our resources and unite our commands if we are to survive. When the Soviets are ready they will cross the Atlantic and invade Europewe must be prepared or we will surely lose. We must mobilize for total war and be ready. We will not get a second chance." The emperor turned to the young sultan who was dressed in BDUs with five stars on his collar and nodded.

"What the emperor says is true. The Soviets intend to enslave and rule the world in their image. A godless communist world, where individuality is frowned on and you live to serve the state. We know the Soviets came over with over 1000 highly trained military personal and technicians and brought lots of equipment with them." Mehmet also knew that the Soviets had a nuclear weapon with them, but so did the Byzantines and he would keep that a secret for now.

"We know that they use thousands of the locals as slaves to build their factories, refineries, ships and run their facilities. That is a weakness we can use. Our people work for the state because they want to live free. We will have to encourage and employ our best and brightest scientists and scholars make new technological advances if we are to survive in this new world. Our allies have found more Soviet equipment as they dig deeper into the Soviet base and find new tunnels that will help us survive against the coming onslaught. This will be a jihad or holy war against the godless communist for both our peoples." The Sultan turned towards Major Jenkins.

"Major Jenkins, please tell us what you have on the drawing board."

"Yes, sir. Jenkins went to the head of the room and pulled open a drape. Behind it was a picture of ship.

"What is that flat top ship?" Asked one of the Ottoman naval officers.

"That's exactly what they are referred as in my time, sir. Or otherwise known as an aircraft carrier. She will be built in the new shipyard in Sinope and named Mehmet II. The Ottomans will provide most of the gold and manpower to build her. We will equip her with 20 aircraft that will carry bombs. She will be 160 meters long and weigh around 12000 tons. We are still are working on the design for her power plants. She will have two steam engines and sail at 15 plus knots." Jenkins turned the picture around and there was a picture of another ship. "This ladies and gentlemen is the Emperor Constantine our first ironclad. She will be 80 meters in length, her beam 17 meters and weigh in at around 5000 tons. She will be both sail and steam powered and expected to make around 12 knots with a 2500hp direct beam engine which will also power the carrier. She will be armed with 50 and 100 pound solid shot and shell firing guns. She will have a crew of 400 men. She will be our test ironclad.

One of the Turkish admirals raised his hand. "Commander

how do you plan to get the armor plate needed to construct such a large ship?"

"Both our empires will have to go on war footing and build factories to forge metal. We have found plans in the Soviet base on how to build metal forges and advanced steam engines which help us immensely. When our expedition returns there are three Russians with them that joined our cause and will help us translate more of the documents we have found."

During Jenkin's speech a messenger walked in and handed the sultan a slip of paper which he quickly read. "Thank you, major." The sultan said. "We just received news that our joint expedition to liberate the holy land has been successful. With the help of our Byzantine allies the Mamelukes have surrendered and decided to become members of the Ottoman Caliphate. In other words I am the final religious authority in Islamic matters. This should prevent any birth of extremism. They have joined their forces with ours. Our forces have also crossed into the red sea and have landed in what will be known as Saudi Arabia to secure Mecca and Medina and our future oilfields."

The sultan turned to the emperor who had walked to the front of the room. "Thank you General. This expedition has now secured our southern flank and a potential oil source. The only problem is it's too far. The Soviets according to what we have been told by General Mavrakis are already refining oil. We have sent an ambassador into Rumania to forge an alliance with the kingdom there and have been successful. We have started building a rail road to Ploesti along the coast through Bulgaria which is also a friendly allied state and a strong trading partner. The distance is about 300 miles and should be completed by the end of the year. Our first leg will be from the coast of Constanta to Ploesti. We will ship the rails and engineers to Rumania. Once oil is transported to the coast we can bring it here by ship here. We will build a refinery on the coast at of the Sea of Marmara. Getting oil from Ploesti is much closer than bringing it from the Middle East. We have also sent feelers to the Venetians but after our campaign in the Mideast and our acquisition of Crete, there is a lot of distrust between our states. I fear the Venetians will not help us. Thus we may not have many allies. We will have to depend on each other. Any questions?"

"Sir, we have heard that your technicians have improved the reloading of ammunition process and are developing a rifle to take a locally developed round."

"Yes, General Gullen. We are now able to reload our ammo with lead bullets. It is not as effective in penetrating power as our modern rounds but it still works. They do foul the barrels rather quickly so a soldier must clean his weapon after use. We are finishing a new infantry rifle design based on the Winchester rifle. It will have a 15 round tubular magazine and a lever to eject the spent casing. We will share this design with you and put it in production along with the ammo we are making for it. Its production will be very manpower intensive, but it's an excellent weapon and will increase our unit fire power immensely."

"Thank you, sir."

"If no one has any other questions will get down to business and begin our staff planning sessions."

Title: Operation Medina™: The Jihad
- Author: George Mavro
- Publisher: TotalRecall Publications, Inc.
- Hardcover, ISBN: 978-1-59095-747-9
- Paperback, ISBN: 978-1-59095-748-6
- eBook ISBN: 978-1-59095-749-3
- Number of pages: 320
- Pubdate: 2011

The Balkans and Mideast, a region very much in the news, is the setting for this action novel which takes place in the not too distant future. The secular pro-western government of Turkey has been overthrown in a violent revolution and replaced by an Islamic fundamentalist regime. Her fanatical leader, General Muhammad Kemal, has contrived a devious plan to restore the Ottoman Empire in the Balkans and unite the Islamic world under his evil rule. To accomplish this, Kemal will launch a devastating war with all the tools in his arsenal including Islamic Jihadist terrorists and WMDs. His first targets are US alley Greece and the few remaining American forces stationed in the region.

For his diabolic scheme to be successful, Kemal must eliminate any source of possible outside interference. To accomplish this, he sends a terrorist team to take out the USAF fighters.

A thousand miles to the south, a Palestinian terrorist sails a boat loaded with anti-ship missiles into Greek waters and delivers a devastating attack in the Mediterranean. The next morning, Turkey and her allies launch a devastating surprise attack against Greece.

With the Greeks facing certain defeat, the U.S. President quickly dispatches to Greece, a fighter squadron and a small USAF Security force contingent for airbase ground defense. The USAF expeditionary force is under the command Lieutenant Colonel Jack Logan a veteran fighter pilot. Logan will be faced with the greatest challenge of his career; he must use every bit of his skills to keep his outnumbered command from being annihilated and help stop the enemy onslaught.

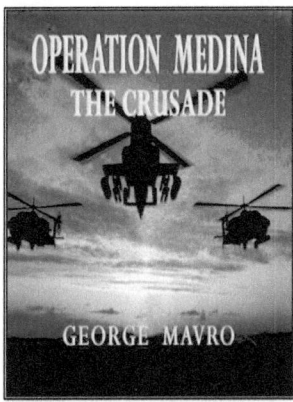

Title: Operation Medina™: The Crusade
- Author: George Mavro
- Publisher: TotalRecall Publications, Inc.
- Hardcover, ISBN: 978-1-59095-663-2
- Paper Back, ISBN: 978-1-59095-664-9
- eBook:, ISBN: 978-1-59095-665-6
- Number of pages: 352
- Pubdate: 2012

The second book of the series Operation Medina, Crusade, opens up with the Greeks retreating on all fronts from the Turkish onslaught. The U.S. has dispatched an expeditionary force consisting of a fighter squadron and a small USAF Security Force to assist the Greeks.

As the Americans join the fight against the Turks, they begin to exact a heavy toll on the enemy. The Greeks manage to stabilize their Albanian and Macedonian fronts, yet are unable to halt the Turks, who continue to push them back. As the tide of battle begins to turn against General Kemal, he plans a final act of madness. A daring plan is formulated involving a simultaneous attack from both air and land to stop the madman from carrying out his deadly scheme. If the plan fails, the Americans will use the only other alternative left to stop him, a B-2 bomber with a nuclear payload which could lead to a nuclear showdown with other Islamic states. With the odds stacked highly against them, the allies must find a way to stop Kemal and avert a nuclear holocaust.

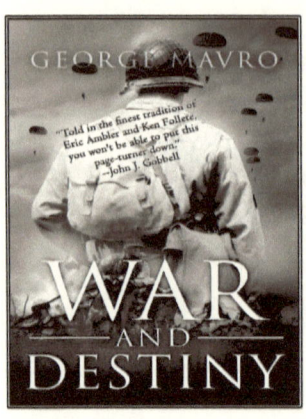

Title: War and Destiny™
- Author: George Mavro
- Publisher: TotalRecall Publications, Inc.
- Hardcover, ISBN: 9781590955710
- Paper Back, ISBN: 9781590955727
- eBook:, ISBN: 9781590955734
- Number of pages: 352
- Pubdate: 2013

When the young New Yorker Markos Androlakis visited the island of Crete in the summer of 1940 for a sabbatical he unwittingly put himself on a trajectory to test the fates of destiny. War soon engulfs the tiny peaceful nation of Greece and she does her best to hold off the Fascist hordes. Markos soon finds himself on the Greek and allied side and fights for survival and for the liberation of his ancestral homeland. War and destiny is an epic tale of war, adventure, intrigue and love.

On 20 May 1941, Germany launched Operation Merkur (Mercury) the largest airborne invasion in history to capture the strategic island of Crete from the allies. . Markos is tasked by the allied commander to help evacuate the Hellenic King to the island's south coast to be transported by the Royal Navy. Unbeknownst to Markos the German Reichsfuhrer Heinrich Himmler has dispatched a ruthless SS officer Georg Mueller to capture the King and return him to Germany. Markos manages to evacuate the king and journeys to Cairo where he is recruited into the US army and the COI which would soon become the OSS, Office of strategic services under the leadership of "Wild Bill Donovan." Markos returns to America to help organize a cadre of Greek American agents to help the Greek resistance fight the ruthless and bloody Nazi occupation.

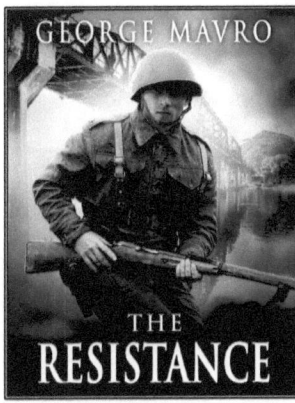

Title: The Resistance™
- Author: George Mavro
- Publisher: TotalRecall Publications, Inc.
- Hardcover, ISBN: 9781590954850
- Paper Back, ISBN: 9781590954867
- eBook:, ISBN: 9781590954874
- Number of pages: 330
- Pubdate: 2013

In the sequel to *War and Destiny* Markos leads his small band of OSS agents into the heart of occupied Greece to strike a decisive blow to the Axis forces occupying his ancestral homeland. His mission to destroy one of the railroad viaducts of the main railroad artery carrying supplies for Rommel's Africa corp. The task almost impossible to do under normal military circumstances will be complicated as he has to get the two major Greek resistance groups, the Royalists and communists to cooperate with each other to carry out this vital mission. Further complicating the mission will be his arch nemesis Standartenführer Georg Muller, a brutal but very efficient Nazi SS officer, who is bent on capturing and killing Markos at any cost. Follow Markos and his team as they try to survive in occupied Europe, during modern history's bloodiest conflict.

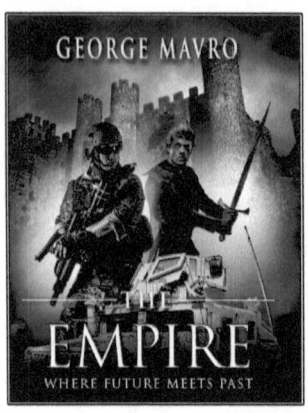

Title: The Empire™
- Author: George Mavro
- Publisher: TotalRecall Publications, Inc.
- Paper Back, ISBN: 9781590954904
- eBook:, ISBN: 9781590954911
- Number of pages: 350
- Pubdate: 2015

While escorting a supply convoy to an off-base communications site north of Bagram Airbase Afghanistan, Master Sergeant George Mavrakis and his team are ambushed by the Taliban. Running for their lives with the few survivors of the ambush they manage to flee to an underground mine, but are trapped inside when a Taliban suicide bomber blows himself up in the entrance, sealing them inside. Traveling deeper into the mine they discover an underground base left there by the Soviets. While exploring the base they find a control room filled with computers and equipment which activated after generator power was restored and a countdown is automatically started.

The arrival of George and his troops from the future have drastically altered the timeline. The Ottoman Sultan Mehmet II will soon put the city of Constantinoplis under siege with over 80,000 troops and 60 huge guns that can tear down the city's walls. In the American's past time line, the Ottomans do capture the city and the emperor is killed in battle. It will be race against time to assist the Byzantines in building up their technical and military capabilities with the skills and knowledge, they brought back from the future, to stop the Ottomans. If they are unsuccessful the future is very bleak for George and his team, whom are lost in time.

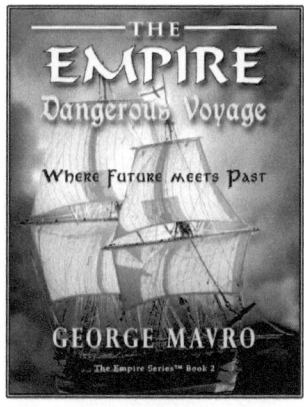

Title: The Empire™ Dangerous Voyage
- Author: George Mavro
- Publisher: TotalRecall Publications, Inc.
- Paper Back, ISBN:
- eBook:, ISBN:
- Number of pages: 256
- Pubdate: 2017

Constantinoplis is surrounded and under siege by the Sultan's 70000 troups. With huge siege canon that can knock down Constantinoplis walls and open a breach for the Ottomans to pour through. Despite the great naval battles, the Byzantine forces have won over the Sultan their future still looks very grim.

The young Sultan has received vital information from his beautiful American prisoner whom he has developed feelings for. He is poised for one last desperate gamble to capture the great city of Constantinople. It will be a do or die attempt. His failure to take the city could result in his own over throw and death.

Can General George Mavrakis with all the technology they have developed for his Byzantine allies stop the massive attack that they know is coming? If they do manage to survive what will the future be and their desire to travel to the world while building their own empire? What does the future have in store for the soldiers lost in the sand of time?

www.ingramcontent.com/pod-product-compliance
Lightning Source LLC
Chambersburg PA
CBHW020627110726
47899CB00002B/675